THE DEADLY LURE
OF GOLD

A JOHN TAILER BISHOP WESTERN ADVENTURE
- BOOK THREE

C. WAYNE WINKLE

1

"You okay, partner?"

Cruz Andrus stood in front of John Bishop, inspecting him from head to toe. His partner shifted his weight from foot to foot, ran his finger around and under the collar of the gleaming white shirt he wore, and glanced around the small room like he was looking for a fast getaway.

"I don't think I've ever been so scared in my entire life," Bishop responded. "Is it too late to run for the hills?"

Cruz grinned at him, his white teeth gleaming against the deep tan of his face. "If you do that, I don't want to be there when Angelina catches up with you. And you know she would."

"Yeah, I know. Is it natural for a feller to be this scared in this kind of situation?"

"How would I know?" Cruz shrugged. "I've never been in this kind of situation before. But you need to just relax. Everything will work itself out without you doing much of anything. I'll be right back."

"Yeah, just relax," Bishop said to his partner's retreating back. "How am I supposed to do that?"

He thought back to a month before. He and Cruz had just returned from finding Riley and Christina Sawyer in Antelope Spring, Arizona Territory. He discovered during that trip that what Cruz had been telling him all along was right. Angelina was the one for him. As soon as they got back, he asked her to meet him in one of the small gardens she liked so well. There, he got down on one knee and asked her to marry him. He said he knew it was fast, but he knew she was the one for him. Angelina told him she'd started working on her wedding dress the day she met him.

That had been a month before. Now, he stood in a small waiting room off the main sanctuary of the Cathedral of St. Francis just off the Plaza in Santa Fe.

Cruz pushed through the small door grinning. "The entire church is full. It looks like most of Santa Fe is here."

Bishop felt his already thumping heart start beating against his ribs as if to bruise them. "Oh, great! You didn't have to tell me that." He paced across the small room and back again. Then she stopped and faced Cruz. "I don't remember when I'm supposed to stand up and when I'm supposed to kneel. I just know I ain't supposed to sit down anytime."

"Don't worry." Cruz slapped him on the shoulder. "Nobody expects you to remember everything. Angelina will be right beside you, and she will let you know what to do. Besides, the ceremony will be in Latin and Spanish, so you won't know what's being said. I suspect as soon as you see Angelina in her dress, none of the rest of it will matter, anyway."

Just then, the door opened again. A young man stuck his head in the open doorway and said, "Senor Bishop, it is time for you to come with me."

Not trusting his voice just then, Bishop nodded and followed the young man. Cruz came close behind.

They entered the main sanctuary of the church through a side door and walked slowly toward the center aisle. The priest stood on a small platform slightly higher than them, smiling down on Bishop as he entered. A glance to his right showed Bishop the church was full, just as Cruz told him. They stopped almost right in front of the priest.

I'd rather face a whole tribe of Indians than have those people watching me, he told himself.

As soon as he stopped in front of the priest, the organ music changed to what Angelina said was the *Bridal Chorus* written by some German man named Wagner. That meant she was getting ready to walk down the aisle toward him.

Everyone in the cathedral stood and looked toward the door.

When Angelina started down the aisle toward him, Bishop lost all his fear of what was going on. She was so beautiful his knees almost gave way. The white of her dress glowed against the duskiness of her skin. Her dark eyes glowed as she locked them onto his. Her smile would've lit up the entire church.

He remembered nothing about the ceremony after she came up beside him.

2

Bishop and Angelina spent their wedding night in a beautiful little casita in the mountains around Santa Fe. The next day, they left for Albuquerque.

As they got ready to leave, Bishop took Angelina in his arms. "I really wish we could go somewhere more fancy than Albuquerque."

"I told you before, I will be happy with you anywhere, John." She kissed him hard on the lips. "As long as I am with you, anywhere will be fine."

They got to Albuquerque late that afternoon. Both of them liked to ride, so they kept their horses at a good pace through the day. After tying their horses in front of the hotel where they'd be staying, they walked in to register.

The first person they saw in the lobby was the Town Marshal. He frowned when he recognized Bishop.

"You again?" the Marshal said, disappointment in his voice.

"Yes, Sir. Me again," Bishop replied with a smile.

"Am I going to have to ask you to leave town this time?" The Marshal had his 'official' expression on.

Angelina stepped up beside Bishop. "Marshal, it sounds like you have had some trouble with my husband in the past."

The Marshal's expression and tone of voice softened some as he tipped his hat to her. "Well, Ma'am, your husband has been around a couple of times when trouble started. I won't say he caused it, but he was in the immediate area when it happened. Both times he left town when I asked him to, and I hope I don't have to do that again."

Angelina put on her best smile. "I assure you, Marshal, he will not cause or be involved in any trouble this time. I will see to it myself." She cut her eyes over at Bishop, who just shrugged.

"I really appreciate that, Ma'am. I will depend on you to keep a rein on him."

"Oh, I will do that. Do not worry."

The Marshal tipped his hat brim to her again and walked out of the hotel with a grin on his face. Angelina turned to Bishop.

"You will have to tell me about your adventures here in Albuquerque some time."

At the end of four days in Albuquerque, Bishop and Angelina sat in a restaurant close to their hotel. They were just finishing their last meal there.

"This has been a good honeymoon," Angelina said to him as she reached over and took his hand.

"Yes it has been," Bishop agreed, squeezing her hand gently.

"There is a woman sitting alone next to the wall who has been looking over here the entire time we have been eating," she said. "She is standing now. I think she is coming here."

A woman slightly older than Bishop came up to their table. She wore a worried expression, her forehead wrinkled so deeply it looked like a plowed field, her eyebrows were almost touching above her nose, and her eyes were bloodshot as if she hadn't been sleeping for several days.

"Excuse me," she said softly. "But you're John Bishop, aren't you?"

Bishop got to his feet holding his napkin. "Yes, Ma'am. That's me. What can I do for you?"

"I would really like to talk to you about my husband, Ernest Thompkins. I'm Lottie Thompkins, by the way." Her voice quivered as if she were just on the verge of tears. "I'm really sorry for interrupting your dinner."

"That's all right, Mrs. Thompkins. Why don't you have a

seat?" He held the chair for her as she sat down. "This is my wife, Angelina." For a moment, he marveled at how good that sounded. His wife!

Resuming his seat, Bishop went on. "Now, what about your husband?"

"Let me say first that I was going to come to Santa Fe and talk with you, but my cousin who works at the desk in the hotel told me you were in town. I hope he won't get in any trouble for telling me that." She paused for a half-second to see if there was any reaction on Bishop's face to this. When she saw none, she went on. "My husband is missing, and I heard about how you find people."

News traveled fast in the West. If it happened close by, that is. It didn't really surprise Bishop that Lottie Thompkins had heard about what he'd done, but he didn't really like all the attention.

Bishop jumped in before she could say anything else. "Well, Mrs. Thompkins, I've found a couple of people, but my wife and I just got married ..."

"Oh, I'm so sorry!" Mrs. Thompkins said. "I thought you were just here on some kind of business or something. If I'd known you were on your honeymoon, I would never have come up to you." A tear leaked out of her left eye and slid down her cheek.

"It's okay, Mrs. Thompkins," Angelina said quickly, leaning toward her. "We don't mind listening to what you have to say, do we, John?"

"Uh, no. No, we don't mind. Why don't you go ahead and tell us about your husband."

"All right. I told you Ernest is missing. Here's what I mean. Six weeks ago, his cousin, Charlie Potts, came to Ernest and convinced him to go on what he called an expedition. This trip was to find gold. The Lost Adams Diggings. He said one of the other men going with him had a map that was supposed to be guaranteed to lead them to that gold."

Bishop interrupted her. "I don't know anything about ... what was it again?"

"The Lost Adams Diggings," Mrs. Thompkins replied.

"I have heard the story," Angelina said. "What I have heard is a man named Adams and about twenty other men found out about a canyon filled with gold. They traveled there, found the gold, and most were killed by Apaches. Adams was lucky to get out alive with a few of his men. The story says the canyon is in the mountains west of Socorro. No one seems to be completely sure where."

"That's about right," Mrs. Thompkins said.

"So your husband and his cousin were goin' to find that gold?" Bishop asked. "There are a lot of mountains west of Socorro, ain't there? Seems like it would be pretty hard to find."

"Charlie said the map that man had showed them right where to go. I don't know where he got the map, but he said it was genuine." Mrs. Thompkins lowered her head and stared at the table for a few seconds. Then she lifted it up again. "We were down on our luck a lot, so Ernest thought it would be a way to start over. But he told Charlie he didn't have any money to chip in or any supplies. Charlie told him not to worry about it, he had everything covered. Now, I don't know how Charlie could've covered everything. He was no more rich than we were. But somehow he did. They were supposed to be gone a month." She paused, drew a deep breath, then let it out. "That was six weeks ago."

"Your husband is two weeks overdue?" Angelina said. "Do you know anything about what happened?"

"No." Mrs. Thompkins shook her head. "Charlie came back a week ago. But he was the only one. He said he got separated from Ernest somehow and couldn't find him. He got hurt in the fighting with the Apaches and didn't remember a lot. He did bring Ernest's diary back with him, though."

Bishop considered what he was going to tell her, knowing she probably knew it anyway. "You realize your husband may be dead, don't you?"

Mrs. Thompkins nodded. "Yes. But I've got to know one way or the other. He might be wandering around on one of those mountains down there, too. Like I said, I've got to know."

Bishop understood her need to know about her husband one way or another, but he wasn't sure about setting out on another manhunt. After all, he'd just gotten married and hadn't even had time to settle down with Angelina. He needed a little time to consider how to tell her that.

"Mrs. Thompkins, you said your husband went on this gold hunt because the two of you were down on your luck. How have you been getting by for the past six weeks?"

"My cousin at the hotel got me a job cleaning the rooms. It doesn't pay much, but I have a place to stay. If you're worried about how I can pay you anything, I'll come up with however much you say somehow."

"No, no." Bishop said quickly. "That's not why I asked. I was just really concerned about how you were surviving."

"You don't have to pay us anything, Mrs. Thompkins," Angelina said. "If we decide to go look for your husband, that is." She cut her eyes at Bishop.

"Uh, yeah, yeah, that's right. If we decide to look for him." Bishop mentally shook himself for not coming right out and telling her that he didn't want to go look for Ernest. At least not now. But he heard himself saying, "I do want to talk to Charlie, though. And find out what he can tell me."

"I can tell you where he lives." Mrs. Thompkins reached into her large bag and brought out a leather-bound book. "This is my husband's diary. Please take it and read it. Maybe it can give you some idea about where he is."

Bishop took the small book. The leather cover was stained and dirty, the edges of the pages almost black.

"I think it got wet somehow," Mrs. Thompkins said. "I

tried to open it up and read it, but the pages are stuck together. I didn't want to destroy it, so I left it alone. Maybe you can dry it out and get the pages apart so you can read it. In any case, I want you to have it. Just bring it back to me. It's almost all I have left of Ernest if he is dead."

"I'll talk with Charlie tomorrow and then let you know," Bishop said. "Even if I don't go lookin' for your husband, I'll see if I can get these pages unstuck so you can read it."

As Mrs. Thompkins got up to leave, Bishop got a glimpse of a large, dark man sitting close by. He looked like he'd been listening and trying hard not to be seen doing so.

3

Bishop rode out to the edge of town and found the little house where Charlie Potts lived. As he rode up to the small house, he noted how it looked like a lot of the other adobe houses in that part of Albuquerque. But still somehow it looked different, too. When he pulled to a stop in front of the house, he took it all in.

The adobe was chipped in a lot of places like someone had thrown something against it from time to time. Here and there across the small yard clumps of weeds grew up through the cracked dirt. Along the front of the property someone had built a sort of picket fence made out of what looked like mesquite limbs. Over the years, some of the limbs rotted and were never replaced, leaving gaps that a person could walk through. The door, once painted a bright blue, now stood washed out almost to a muddy white.

Bishop dismounted, tied Streak to one of the fence sticks, and walked up to the door. When he knocked, he could feel the door almost swaying just from the force of his knocks.

In a few seconds, the door was opened slowly, and a man stood there staring at him. A blood-stained bandage on the side of his head over his left ear was held in place by a strip of cloth. The man wore no shirt, only the top of his long johns that had once been red, but now were a light pink. Sweat rings stained them under his arms and around his neck. His pants were baggy canvas ones stuffed into the tops of mule ear boots. His hair that wasn't covered by the bandage stuck out at odd angles from his head as if he'd been asleep and moving around a lot. No razor had touched his cheeks for at least a week. The eyes that stared at Bishop were dark enough to qualify as black along with his hair.

"Are you Charlie Potts?" Bishop asked after the two of them stared at each other for several seconds.

"Yeah. Who're you?" Potts' words spat out of his mouth as if they tasted bad.

"John Bishop. Mrs. Thompkins sent me to talk to you."

"Oh, yeah. You're the manhunter." Potts stepped aside. "Come on in."

It took Bishop's eyes a moment to adjust to the dim

interior of the small house. It was basically one fair-sized room with an alcove partitioned off with a blanket hanging from pegs in the walls. He figured that was the sleeping space. Over to his left was a small area that served as a kitchen. It was little more than a shelf fastened to the wall close by the Spanish style fireplace that served as stove and heat source for the house.

"Have a seat." Potts motioned to the table in the middle of the floor. Three mismatched chairs stood around it. He took one of them and sat down.

After Bishop pulled out one of the chairs and sat down, Potts said, "Lottie said she'd asked you to find Ernest for her. I guess you're here to see what I can tell you about where he might be."

Potts paused then as if expecting an answer, even though what he said wasn't a question. Bishop just nodded.

Potts took the time to pull out the makings and roll a cigarette. During the ceremony of thumbing out a sheet of thin paper, using his thumb and forefinger to pull out tobacco from a pouch and make sure it was evenly distributed on the paper, rolling the smoke tightly, licking the end of the paper to make it stick, then scraping a lucifer along the top of the table, and getting the cigarette going, he didn't look at Bishop. Once he had a good draw on the cigarette, he blew the smoke toward the ceiling, then lowered his eyes to Bishop's face.

"Well, Mr. Manhunter, there ain't much I can tell you

other than what Lottie's prob'ly already told you." He let the cigarette hang from the corner of his mouth and stared at Bishop through the smoke. "There's a lot I don't remember since I got this." He pointed at the bandage.

During this whole procedure, Bishop never took his eyes off Potts. He was beginning to think there wasn't a whole lot to like about the man.

"Why don't you just start at the beginnin' and tell me what happened. I'll ignore the parts that Mrs. Thompkins already told me."

Potts shrugged, took another drag, and let the smoke come out between his words. "I talked to Ernest about goin' to find that gold 'cause I knew they were down on their luck. Me'n four other men were goin' anyway, so he'd be one more gun if we needed one. We went out, didn't find no gold, but did find Apaches. The men with me got killed, and I got separated from Ernest. Couldn't find him. Got shot, but somehow I got back, they didn't. That's about it."

When it was clear Potts had no more to say, Bishop nodded. "Who were the other four men with you?"

Potts stared at him again, one eye squinted against the smoke from his cigarette. "Arthur Ripley, Dawson McAlister, Dixon Howard, and Nolan Sharpe. All people I knew." He didn't elaborate on how he knew the men.

"Who had the map?"

From the narrowing of his other eye, Potts showed Bishop his surprise. "So you know about the map, too.

Sharpe had it. Wouldn't never say where he got it or even show it to us. Just said it was supposed to be genuine." He snorted through his nose. "From the beginnin' I was doubtful it was any good. We went from one mountain to another. Never did find any gold."

"Was there anybody else with you?"

Potts hesitated, then said, "Yeah, there was a half-Apache guide, Alito."

Again, Bishop found himself having to ask specific questions to get any answers. "There was an Apache guide, too? Who's idea what that?"

"Sharpe's. I never did figger out why we needed a guide when he had that map. But I never did see that Indian guide us at all, unless it right to those other Apaches. Oh, he talked to Sharpe ever' once in a while, but I never did trust him."

"Thompkins didn't have to get any of his own supplies," Bishop said. "Mrs. Thompkins said you told him not to worry about that. Where did all the money for supplies come from?"

Potts shrugged. "I don't know. When Sharpe came to me with the idea, he said all of the supplies we'd need had already been bought. He said we would talk about payin' our share for 'em once we found that gold."

"So this Sharpe feller must've had money then?" Bishop framed this as a question.

"That was the funny part. I've known Sharpe for a long

time, and never did he have that much money. I don't know where it came from."

"What about Thompkins' diary? How did you come to have that?"

"He must've dropped it or somethin' that last time we had a run-in with Apaches. Just before we got separated. I found it, knew Lottie would want it, so I brought it back to her."

"You read any of it?"

Another snort from Potts. "I can't read. Never went to school. Not for any length of time anyway. I always found somethin' more interestin' to do. Besides, the pages are all stuck together since it got wet."

Bishop pondered on what he'd heard from Potts, not liking the man, but not able to put his finger on why exactly. He'd learned very little really. From the way Potts acted, he thought there was some, maybe a lot, that the man hadn't told him.

"I guess you were pretty lucky to get back alive when none of the others did."

Potts took a long drag off his cigarette, blew the smoke toward the ceiling again, and took his time answering the implied question. "It had to be luck. That's all it could have been, 'cause I'm not all that good a fighter. And I don't remember much about how I got back or any of it, really. I reckon gettin' shot in the head like this had somethin' to do with that."

"How did you get shot?"

Potts shrugged. "Must've been in that last fight with the Apaches. The one where I got separated from Ernest. I just remember the blow, then nothin' until I got back home. I don't know how I got away from the Apaches or much else about that whole trip. I don't even know for sure where we were when me and Ernest got separated."

"That wound is that bad, huh?"

"The sawbones here said it was a deep cut just above my ear. Any deeper and I'd be dead. He said people sometimes lose their memory for things that happen around the time of gettin' wounded like this. He said he'd seen a lot of that in the war. Sometimes people start rememberin' things after a while, but sometimes they don't."

"I saw some of that in the war, too. I think sometimes things jogged those men's memories, too. But not always."

"Yeah, well, it ain't too much fun not rememberin' things, especially important things." Potts got busy rolling another cigarette.

Bishop got to his feet, not thinking he would get much more from Potts. "Thanks for your help."

"You goin' to go look for Ernest?"

"I might. I ain't decided for sure yet." With that, he left the little house and its not-so-helpful inhabitant.

As soon as he stepped outside, Bishop got a glimpse of a man riding around a bend in the street. The man looked like the same one who had been listening to his conversation with Mrs. Thompkins.

4

After talking with Charlie Potts, Bishop rode Streak back to the hotel where he and Angelina stayed. He didn't think about the man he saw as he rode back.

He tied Streak to the hitch rail outside the hotel and got right in front of him. "Now, I expect you to act right, and you know what I mean. Don't you do anything to anybody's horse if they tie him up next to you. It's not important that you make sure ever'body knows you're the boss. You know that, so that's enough."

Streak stared into Bishop's eyes for a few seconds, then looked away. As he did, he snorted through his nose. Bishop wasn't sure whether that was his mule's way of letting him know he'd do whatever he wanted or if he was agreeing to behave himself. But he suspected it was the former.

Stepping up onto the porch that fronted the hotel, Bishop glanced down the street. Tied there was a dark-colored horse with one white stocking that he thought looked like the one he saw the man riding away from Potts' house earlier. He just filed that away and went on inside.

Nodding at the young man behind the registration desk, he climbed the stairs to their room on the second floor. Angelina sat beside the open window that looked down on the street.

"I saw you ride in," she said as she lifted her face for a kiss.

Bishop kissed her deeply. *I could get used to this,* he realized. *I really could.* "Had a talk with Ernest Thompkins' cousin, Charlie Potts. He didn't tell me much that Mrs. Thompkins didn't say last night. But I got the feelin' he wasn't tellin' ever'thing." He sat down on the edge of the bed. "There was somethin' about him that I didn't care much for, too. Don't know for sure what it was, but I just didn't like the man."

"Didn't like him or just not sure about him?"

Bishop shook his head. "Just didn't like him. Somethin' that I can't put a finger on, but it's there all the same." He paused, looked out the window for a few seconds, then went on. "I told Mrs. Thompkins that I'd let her know about goin' to look for her husband after I talked with

Potts. I'll go find her and let her know that I'll go and see if I can find him."

"Good!" Angelina stood from the chair by the window. "This should be a great adventure. When do we leave?"

Bishop stared up at her. "Now, hold on! Don't get the idea that you're goin', too. This won't be any place for a woman. I'll send for Cruz to come and go with me."

Angelina stood up straighter, her brow wrinkling, her eyes almost literally sparking. With her hands on her hips, she said, "Of course I'm going with you. You're my husband, so wherever you go, I go."

Bishop stood, shaking his head. "It's goin' to be a whole lot too dangerous for you to go with me. There's goin' to be rough ridin', sleepin' on the ground, and who knows what kinds of animals we might run into. Not to mention Apaches. No. You just can't go. It's too dangerous."

He had barely finished talking when Angelina spouted out a rapid torrent of Spanish. She went on for a long minute, her eyebrows drawn together until they almost touched over her nose.

Bishop frowned also and held up his hands, palms toward her. "Wait, wait! Slow down and speak English. What are you sayin'?"

"I am saying that you are a stubborn man who does not know when just to agree with me and accept that I am right. And I am telling you that I will tend to your hurts and cook for you while we go on this adventure together. So you should just agree that I will go with you."

For a few seconds, he didn't know what to say. Then he said, "I'm goin' to get Cruz to go with me. He can cook." As a way to convince her not to go, it was lame, and he knew it.

"I can cook better than Cruz. You know that. Besides, you will need him to help you look. With me there, you can get more done." Her tone of voice told him she thought the matter was settled.

Bishop came up with another reason for her not to go. "If you go, I'll be worryin' about keepin' you safe the whole time."

"You will be worrying about keeping yourself and Cruz safe anyway, so I won't add to your worry." She smiled then. The smile that always hit him right between the eyes. "And not only will I take care of your injuries, I will keep you warm at night. Cruz won't do that, will he?"

Bishop could think of nothing else to say no matter how much as he wanted to. He opened his mouth a couple of times, but nothing would come out.

Angelina smiled again and batted her eyes at him.

"All right," he said with a sigh after a few moments. "But you've got to do just what I say and keep a close watch the whole time."

"I will do that, my husband." She stepped up to him, put her arms around him, and kissed him. "I always do just what you say. That is what a good wife does, is it not?"

Somehow, Bishop knew she didn't mean those last words she said. He knew she would listen to him, then do what she thought best. And he knew it would do no good to argue.

"All right, let's go find Mrs. Thompkins and tell her we'll go find her husband. I'll wire Cruz to meet us either on the way to Socorro or when we get there."

Downstairs, they found Mrs. Thompkins standing by the desk, talking to her cousin. Charlie Potts stood with them. She looked up at them as they came down the stairs.

"Mrs. Thompkins, we've decided to go look for your husband," Bishop told her.

"Oh, thank you, thank you," she said, swiping away a tear. "I'm so glad you decided to help me. Charlie here has just told me he's going back out there to see if he can find Ernest. This way, you can go together."

Potts stared at Bishop with a sort of triumphant gleam in his eyes. Then he cut his gaze over at Angelina and something very different shone in them. Something Bishop didn't like at all.

Mrs. Thompkins went on speaking. "I've managed to scrape together a little money to help pay for the supplies you'll need. Charlie will get his own."

"You don't need to be concerned about our supplies, Mrs. Thompkins," Bishop said. "We'll take care of gettin' those ourselves. I plan to leave in the mornin', not long after sunrise." He directed this next directly to Potts. "Can you make it that early and be ready to go?"

"Don't worry about me. I'll be here and ready."

"Okay." Bishop tipped his hat to Mrs. Thompkins. "Me and Angelina have some things to attend to, so we'll see you later."

When they were out of earshot of Charlie and Mrs. Thompkins, Angelina said, "I see what you mean about Charlie Potts. He is not a likeable man. I did not like the way he looked at me."

"Neither did I. I may have to have a talk with him about that before long."

"Just do not hurt him too much, my husband. And if he tries anything with me, I will take care of him."

"I have no doubt you will. I pity the man who gets on your bad side."

She took his arm and squeezed it against her. "Just be sure to remember that yourself."

"Yes, Ma'am. I'll do that. Let's stop in the telegraph office and send wire to Cruz."

5

That night, before climbing into bed, Bishop took out the leather-bound diary that Lottie Thompkins had given him. The one Potts said he found when he got separated from Thompkins. On the inside of the front cover, an inscription written in a feminine hand showed the diary was given to Thompkins by his wife several years before. The ink was smudged and faded.

Must've been when they had money for such things, Bishop realized. *Wonder what happened to drag 'em down to where Thompkins was desperate enough to go on a hunt for lost gold? Whatever it was, at least this inscription tells me this really was Ernest Thompkins' diary.*

He turned to the first page of the diary and saw a completely different hand had written in the diary. Written in pencil, some of the pages were smudged, but the words were readable. It took a lot of concentration and a little guessing. He turned to the back of the diary and noticed some pages had been torn out. Then he turned to the front again. He managed to separate some of the pages. All of those had some writing on them. He turned back to the first page and began reading.

This is the first night out from Albuquerque. We got a later start than I thought we would because one of the men with Charlie forgot to bring a canteen, so we had to go back and let him buy one. I'm surprised that Dawson, the man who forgot his canteen, is even going with us. He doesn't seem the type who enjoys the outdoors much. Charlie said he's a store owner in Albuquerque.

The other men with us are Arthur, Dixon, and Nolan. I forget their last names, but that's not a problem. They all seem to be fine men. All of us are eager to get out into the mountains and find the gold that's supposed to literally be laying on the ground somewhere out there. Nolan has a map which he says is genuine. He hasn't said where or how he got it. There's some writing on the back of the map, but he's only given any of us a glimpse of the map or the writing. Charlie says not to worry about it, he trusts Nolan.

I've always been suspicious of people who say they have the map of where such and such can be found. If we weren't so far down on our luck, I wouldn't even be out here with these men. But Lottie deserves more than I can give her right now, so here I am. If there's even a little chance I'll find some gold to help us get back on our feet, then I'm willing to try.

Around the fire tonight, we talked about how we'd split up any gold we find. After some discussion, we decided to split it almost equally. But Nolan will get a little more than the rest of us because he has the map and furnished all the supplies we have. Nobody's said where he got the money for the supplies, and I'm not going to ask. The weight of the gold was brought up. Gold is really heavy, so we might not be able to carry much of it out with us. We talked about hiding it somewhere and coming back for it later.

I sort of feel out of place in this bunch. All of them know each other from somewhere, and I don't know any of them other than Charlie. But nobody seems to care. We all know that what we're doing might be dangerous, too, because of the Indians out there. So me being along is one more gun if we need it.

Something happened tonight just about dark. A man came into camp from the dark. He's half-Apache by the name of Alito. Charlie says Nolan hired him as a guide. I wanted to ask why we need a guide when we've got that map, but I didn't say anything. I don't like Alito. He looks at all of us like a wolf looking at jackrabbits. I don't know why I think that, maybe because he's half-Apache. But I'll keep my distance from him anyway.

The diary entry for that day ended there. Bishop wondered about the man with the map and where he got it. And about how he bought all of the supplies a group that large would need. The idea of having a half-Apache guide also struck him as odd. It was something he'd have to talk more to Charlie about the next morning.

That caused him to ponder on Charlie going along with them. On one hand, it would be a good idea to have him go along to show where the group went before being attacked. At least as much as he could remember. It wasn't clear how much he remembered before being shot. But he'd have to be sure to watch him around Angelina.

6

The next morning, Bishop sat in the restaurant next to the hotel having just finished breakfast when he saw Charlie Potts ride up. Halfway surprised that the man actually got up and made it to the hotel before daylight, he pushed away from the table and walked outside.

"I see you made it in time to leave with us," he said casually as he walked up to Charlie. "I wanted to ask you about something. Last night I read some in your cousin's diary. He mentioned that half-Apache guide that was with your expedition. Tell me again why would you need a guide when you had that map?"

Charlie stopped fiddling with the cinch on his saddle and stared at Bishop for a few seconds. Finally, he said, "It was Nolan Sharpe's idea to have Alito come with us. He said it wouldn't hurt to have somebody who had actually been in the mountains. The map was good, but didn't show all the details or the best way to get from one place to the other. It don't really matter anyhow. That Indian is either dead now or with the Apaches."

"So you think maybe he had somethin' to do with you runnin' into the Apaches that killed the other men?"

"Lookin' back at it now, that seems reasonable."

Bishop nodded. "Okay, that makes sense I guess. I was just curious. We'll be ready to go in a few minutes."

Back inside the restaurant, Bishop ordered one more cup of coffee and sat back down at his table. He noticed the same man who had been listening in to what Mrs. Thompkins told them. That man was sitting across the room against the wall. Bishop didn't remember seeing him before. At the same time that his coffee was brought to the table, the man stood and walked over to Bishop.

"Mind if I sit down?"

The man's voice matched his size. His voice sounded like it came from the bottom of a whiskey barrel, and his chest looked to be just about as large as that barrel. The man wore all black clothing, including the gun belt and holster that held a Colt Peacemaker on his right hip. His hair and the short, well-trimmed beard were both black as well. Only his eyes were different. They were a very dark blue. And he had a way of looking directly into Bishop's eyes without blinking that made it seem he could see all the way inside Bishop's head.

Bishop nodded at the empty chair across from him. "Sure, why not?" In fact, he wanted to know what this man was after.

"My name's Daniel Upton." He paused as if waiting for some recognition from Bishop. When he didn't get it, he went on with a little edge to his voice. "You're John Bishop, I understand. And you've told Mrs. Thompkins that you're going to look for her husband."

When Upton paused this time, Bishop responded. "Seems like you know a lot that might not concern you. What business is it of yours whether I'm goin' to look for Mr. Thompkins?"

Whether Bishop's attitude bothered Upton or not, nothing showed on that face that looked like it might've been carved from some hundred-year-old oak. "I thought you need to know some more of the story. I invested a lot of money in that expedition. Money for all the supplies that Nolan Sharpe bought. That map he had? I gave it to him. It's the real article. It showed right where they needed to go. And like all investors, I expected a profit from the money I gave Sharpe. But I've gotten nothing."

"Why didn't you go lookin' for that gold yourself? It wouldn't have cost you as much to do that as it did payin' for all those supplies for so many men."

"Let's just say I had some other business I had to take

care of and couldn't go. In any case, I would've gotten the money back plus more with the gold."

Bishop jumped in. "It was my understandin' that they didn't get any gold, if that's what you expected."

A snort and a grim smile under the black mustache came after Bishop said this. "I suspect Sharpe and Potts and the others found gold all right. Found it and hid it so I wouldn't know. Potts came back and told me they didn't find any, but I don't believe him."

So Potts knew about this Upton feller after all. He knew enough to come back and report to him, at least. He didn't bother to tell me that. I wonder if maybe he did what Upton said and found some gold, then hid it. If he did, was Thompkins in on it, like Upton thinks?

All this flashed through Bishop's mind as he listened to Upton go on.

"Now, I've got a proposition for you," Upton said, his voice changing just enough for Bishop to hear. He began sounding like a conspirator talking to an associate. "I know Lottie Thompkins gave you a diary that her husband kept. I saw her hand it to you. I want that diary. It might have some information in it that would tell me for sure if they found gold and hid it from me. It could tell me where they might've hidden it. I'll give you $500 for it right now."

"That's a lot of money for somethin' that might or might not tell you what you want to know," Bishop said. "Anyhow,

I got to say no. It ain't mine to sell. It belongs to Mrs. Thompkins."

"No matter who it belongs to, you have possession of it," Upton replied. "I'll give you $1000 for it. Nobody has to know."

"A thousand dollars!" Bishop raised his eyebrows for effect. "That's a lot of money. You want that diary real bad, Upton. Makes me wonder if there's somethin' in there you don't want other people to see. My answer's still no. Besides, Mrs. Thompkins wants it back after I find out what happened to her husband. It's about all she has left of him."

Upton sat back in his chair. He'd been leaning over the table the whole time, basically getting in Bishop's face. It had worked before with others, intimidating them with his size. He breathed heavily through his nose.

"I couldn't care less about Mrs. Thompkins and what she has left of her husband. You're trying to get more money from me, I see. Well, it's not going to work. I was hoping we could come to a business agreement like gentlemen, but I see I misjudged you." Upton stood, glaring down at Bishop. "You need to bear in mind, Bishop, that I will get what I want. I always do. One way or another."

With that, Upton turned on his heel and glided from the restaurant. Bishop never heard his boots hit the floor as he walked quickly away.

That feller will be a real bad enemy, I suspect, he told himself.

He finished his coffee and went upstairs to pack the rest of what he would take with him. Angelina was ready to go when he got there. Ten minutes later, they walked back downstairs and out to her horse, Streak, and the pack horse they would use. Potts stood there on the porch smoking a cigarette.

"Ready to go?" Bishop asked as he passed the man.

"Yeah. I'm waitin' on you." Potts went to his horse and pack horse. Both of them appeared to be well cared-for and able to take on the trip that faced them.

Bishop finished packing his and Angelina's things on their pack horse, then climbed on board Streak. When he was settled in the saddle, he asked Potts, "Why didn't you tell me about Daniel Upton?"

Potts hesitated in tightening the cinch on his saddle, just for a second. Clearly, he hadn't expected Bishop to bring the man up. "I didn't think he was important," Potts finally replied.

"He claims he was the man who supplied that map and paid for all the supplies you boys had on your expedition," Bishop said. "But you didn't think he was important?"

Potts put a foot in the stirrup and hoisted himself aboard his horse. Then he turned to face Bishop. "I didn't know Upton paid for ever'thing until after I got back. I guess I just forgot about him when we were talkin'."

"Sounds like you really didn't think he was important,

but you reported to him about not findin' any gold when you got back. That sounds to me like you knew him better than you let on."

Potts looked up the street, then down at the ground under the horse's feet. When he raised his head up, he didn't look directly into Bishop's eyes. "Look, the man came out to my house right after I got back. I wouldn't let him in, because he looked scary. He told me about puttin' a lot of money into our expedition, but I remember Nolan Sharpe tellin' us about him. Sharpe said Upton is just jealous because he, Sharpe, got the money together to go find that gold. Upton is another treasure hunter and wanted to find that gold himself, but couldn't get anybody to go with him. He's a liar. That's all there is to it. Now, can we get on with our trip?"

"Sure." Bishop knew he wasn't going to get any more out of Potts just then. He hung back, letting the man lead out. *Wonder who's lyin' here? Is it Upton, Sharpe, or maybe Potts? Somebody surely is.*

"What was that all about?" Angelina asked, coming up beside him.

He told her about the conversation he had with Upton and how he thought the man would be trouble. "It's not too late for you to stay here while I'm gone," he said, knowing what her answer would be.

"I'm not the kind of woman who watches her husband

ride off possibly into trouble, then stays home and worries about him. I'm with you all the way. You won't get rid of me that easily."

As she rode off ahead of him, Bishop watched her proudly.

7

They took it easy that first day out, stopping a couple of times to make sure the pack horses were doing okay. It wouldn't do for one of them to develop a sore on its back from a loose pack that slipped every time it took a step. They would need all of the supplies on both horses for that trip. And Bishop didn't know how well Potts had loaded his pack horse until he saw for himself.

That night they made their first camp on the bank of the Rio Grande River where there was grass for the animals, trees for firewood, and a clay bank to build their fire against. Bishop stood out with Streak, brushing him down a second time when the mule's head came up. He looked out into the dusk that was just beginning to leak out of the canyons and ravines to cover the land and make way for night. The sun had just slipped below the western horizon and had splashed the sky with the red wash it left behind.

Bishop held Streak's nose so he wouldn't make any sound and listened. Soon he heard the sound of an approaching horse coming toward the camp. Not knowing who the rider might be, he drew his Remington and waited.

The rider kept coming right toward the camp, so there was no mistaking his intent. Maybe it was just a lonely traveler who saw their fire and thought he might get a cup of coffee or a meal. That happened often enough out in the wilderness.

As Bishop listened, the rider rode up and stopped just outside the light from the fire. He saw that both Angelina, who was cooking, and Potts had heard the man ride up.

"Hello, the fire!" the man called out. "Can I ride in?"

"Come on in," Potts called back. "I've been waitin' for you."

Waiting for him? Bishop said to himself. *Who was it that Potts was waiting for?*

Bishop walked back toward the fire, Remington ready in his hand. The man rode on into the light and dismounted. Potts came up to him and shook his hand.

When Bishop walked up behind him, the new man whirled around, his hand starting for the gun on his right hip. He stopped abruptly when he saw the Remington not quite pointed at his belly.

"Who's this?" Bishop asked.

"His name's Greer," Potts answered. "I asked him to come with us. He knows Apache, so I thought he might be handy if we have to talk to any of 'em."

"It would've been nice to know about this before now. Some of the time when strange men show up, there's trouble because not ever'body's been informed." Bishop dropped the Remington back into its holster. He didn't offer his hand for the man to shake.

"If I'm goin' to cause problems," Greer said, "I can go my way."

"No, no. It'll be okay." Potts smiled at the newcomer. "Ever'thing will be okay."

Bishop turned his back on Greer and went back to Streak to continue brushing him. In a minute, Greer brought his horse out and staked it along with the other horses. When he came back to return to the fire, Streak stuck his rump out in the man's way. It wasn't that he meant to. At least, Bishop didn't think so, but it caused Greer to stumble a little. When Greer shoved Streak's rump out of the way, he got kicked for his trouble.

"You need to control that mule," Greer said through gritted teeth as he rubbed his shin where Streak had grazed it with his hoof. "I might have to shoot it if it gets in my way."

Bishop stopped his brushing and leaned against Streak, meeting Greer's eyes in the dusk. "Mister, if you try to do anything to this mule, I'll tie you down on the ground and let him do what he wants with you. Then if there's anything left of you, I'll finish you off myself."

Greer held Bishop's gaze for a second, then looked away, turned, and walked on to the fire. Bishop watched him go.

"Now, that wasn't a very nice thing for you to do to a stranger," he told Streak once Greer was out of earshot. "Do I have to tell you all the time to behave yourself?"

Streak responded with one his loudest farts.

Bishop finished brushing him, then staked Streak out with the horses. For a few more seconds he stood in the gathering darkness looking up at the stars that filled the sky. That was something he often did when he was out away from civilization because he could see so many of the tiny dots up in the night sky. Lowering his gaze out to the area around them, he spotted another light in the distance. It was too low down to be another star.

A fire gleamed out there. It looked like it was a long way behind them, but distances at night were tricky. It was probably just another traveler out on the main trail between Albuquerque and Socorro. He knew it wasn't Cruz. His partner wouldn't catch up to them this soon.

8

Bishop's sleep that night was fitful, full of dreams about gold, Apaches, and people lying to him about nothing important, just lying to be lying. Once, Angelina shook him awake.

"What is wrong?" she asked, her brow wrinkled. "You were tossing and turning, mumbling something about liars."

"Just bad dreams, that's all." He took her hand and brought it to his mouth for a kiss. "I'm sorry to keep you awake. Sometimes I have those dreams about the war."

She snuggled closer to him. "Just put your arms around me and forget about everything else. That will help you sleep better."

And it did.

The next day they rode along the west bank of the Rio Grande River on their way to Socorro. About mid-morning, Greer turned in his saddle and scanned the trail behind them.

"Somebody's comin'," he said to all of them.

Potts had been in the lead and stopped when Greer pointed to the small dust cloud behind them. "Looks like only one or two people under that dust. Prob'ly just other travelers comin' down the trail, but why don't we pull off and wait to see?"

They rode off the trail and into a small stand of mesquite trees. As they watched the dust cloud come on closer, it became clear there was only one rider under it. Soon, the distant image of the rider could be made out, but not who it was specifically.

"That may be my partner," Bishop told Potts and Greer. "I sent for him before we left Albuquerque."

"Didn't know you had a partner," Potts said.

Bishop turned to face him. "There may be a lot you don't know about me." Then he turned back to watch the rider get closer. When he could be sure, he said, "Yep, that's Cruz all right." He rode out onto the trail to meet Cruz.

"I thought that dust I saw ahead of me might be you," Cruz said when he pulled even with Bishop. "But it was more than I thought you'd make."

"We've got some folks with us."

"You said 'we'. Don't tell me Angelina is with you." Cruz grinned at this.

"She is. I tried to talk her out of goin', but you know how she is. The other two are Charlie Potts, Thompkins' cousin, and a feller named Greer that Potts told to come along. He's supposed to be able to talk to Apaches."

"This Greer a half-breed?" Cruz asked, his voice betraying his dislike of the man.

"Yeah, looks like he is. Why? What do you know about him?"

"I've heard of him, that's all. And not very much I've heard is good. He's one to watch."

By that time, the others had come out to meet Cruz. Bishop made the introductions. He noticed a distinct lack of enthusiasm when he introduced Greer to Cruz.

Before they got underway again, Cruz said, "I came across some fresh tracks back about two miles. They crossed your trail and went on into the hills. Shod horses, only two I think, so I think it was prob'ly a white man. I kinda wondered about him crossing the trail and not staying on the main trail."

No one said anything, but Bishop remembered seeing the other fire the night before. It could've been a couple of miles behind them. He dismissed it as just one of those strange things that sometimes happens out on the trail.

"We can make it to Socorro before sundown if we get back on the way," Potts suggested.

When he reined his horse around and started south on the trail, the others followed. Bishop and Cruz brought up the rear with Angelina just in front of them.

"From what you said in your telegram, I figgered it would just be me'n you on this trip," Cruz said.

"Yeah, I thought the same thing. Thought we could ride in real quiet, find out what happened to Thompkins, and ride back out. Even with Angelina along, we could've done that. Then, Potts said he'd come and guide us to the places he'd been with Thompkins. Greer was a surprise. And there's one other thing. A feller named Upton talked to me about wantin' to buy the diary I've got. Said he'd put up a lot of money for that first expedition. Got real mad when I told him I wouldn't sell the diary. Potts said he was lyin', that he didn't put up any money." Bishop paused long enough to study their back trail, then went on. "I know somebody's lyin' about some things, but I don't know for sure who."

"Sounds like it might be best not to trust anybody except the three of us," Cruz said, nodding to include Angelina.

"Yeah, I think you're prob'ly right."

They rode down the small main street of Socorro, population about 550, about an hour before sundown. The town sat slightly off the main trail that went on down toward Hot Springs, New Mexico Territory. As towns went, it was about average. Several false-fronted stores lined the street on both sides. The town boasted three saloons along the short street.

They passed the saloons and headed for the only hotel. Since they were staying the night, Bishop wanted to spend it sleeping in a relatively good bed. For the next several days, they'd be sleeping on the ground. Both Potts and Greer opted for sleeping in the livery stable.

Once they were unpacked and in their rooms, Bishop, Angelina, and Cruz took their horses to the livery stable and paid the man there for taking care of them. Then they headed for the only restaurant in town.

The restaurant was attached to one of the saloons. From the outside, the saloon looked like the best of the three. Inside, the restaurant was open to the saloon all the way along one side. It wasn't the best set-up Bishop had seen, but the other choice as far as eating was concerned would be to cook something for themselves somewhere. They'd be doing that soon enough, so they decided to go on in.

Just inside the door, they stopped and looked around for a table. With the nearness of the saloon, the noise level inside was high. More people than Bishop would've thought would be eating in a restaurant in a small town were there. Most of them settled in on the saloon side of the building. In order to get to a table, they had to walk along the nonexistent dividing line between saloon and restaurant.

Bishop pointed to a table toward the back of the room and started that way. Angelina followed him, with Cruz coming up last.

Several of the men sitting at the tables on the saloon side turned to look at Angelina. She had to pass right next to a table where a man sat who paid a lot of attention to her.

When she was right beside him, he reached out and grabbed her around the waist. "Come here, Honey," he said loudly. "You need to spend some time with me." His grin was very suggestive.

Angelina struggled against his grip, finally breaking free momentarily. "I do not wish to get close enough to you to get past your smell," she said.

The man was quick and grabbed her again. "You got a mouth on you, Honey. I like that. Come and set on my lap."

Angelina grabbed the little finger on his left hand and began bending it backward. When it got almost to the breaking point, the man yelled and let her go.

Several things happened almost at once then. First, Angelina stumbled a couple of steps away from the man. Next, the man shook his left hand while he cussed like a drunken sailor. Then, he started to push himself up from the chair and come after Angelina.

By that time, she had regained her balance, produced a .36 caliber Colt Pocket Revolver Model 1849 that no one knew she had, and cocked the pistol. She pointed the pistol right at the man and fired. The bullet blew a hole in the seat of his chair about three inches from his crotch. The man froze immediately, his mouth open in shock.

Both sides of the establishment went silent at the blast of the pistol being fired. Everyone turned to see what was happening.

"You, you be careful with that gun, Lady," the man said, his face having drained of all color. He stayed in a sort of half-in, half-out crouch in the chair with his hands on the arms supporting him.

"I have every intention of being careful with this gun," Angelina replied. "That shot went right where I wanted it to. The next one will be just a few inches higher." She paused to let the man grasp what she was saying. "Now," she went on, "you will sit back down and keep your hands to yourself. Okay?"

"Y-yes, Ma'am," the man said. If he'd been drunk before, he was surely sober now.

"Very good. Now, I am going with my husband and my friend to have our dinner. You stay right there." Saying this, she backed away from the man, keeping the pistol in her hand.

When she got to the table where Bishop stood holding

her chair out for her, he said, "I didn't know you had that pistol."

"It is one my grandfather gave me," she replied. "He said it was good for snakes and varmints. It looks like he was right."

9

After supper, Bishop and Angelina went back to their room. They planned to get an early start the next morning, so they wanted to get a good night's sleep. Bishop tossed and turned for several minutes before getting up and sitting on the side of the bed.

So he wouldn't keep Angelina awake, he picked up the diary and decided to read for a while. He turned the oil lamp up just enough for him to be able to read. Carefully, he peeled some more pages apart and noted how the words, written in pencil, were faded but could be read if he held the page up close to the light. The next entry started off on a fresh page.

Our second night on the trail to finding the lost gold. Even though it's hard being away from Lottie, I keep myself from feeling bad by reminding myself that this is for us. To give us a way to get back on our feet. She deserves it, so my feeling a little uncomfortable is not too much to go through.

Everyone still is excited about this expedition. I know there will probably be some trouble among us at some point, but I'm sure we can work it out. If for no other reason, than working it out will allow us to get the gold we're after.

Nolan still won't show us the map, but still assures us it is genuine. He doesn't seem to doubt it at all. I'm still not completely sure. If someone had a map that showed where to find a canyon full of gold, why wouldn't that person go get it for himself? I don't have an answer for that, so I still wonder about the map. No one else seems concerned.

Tonight around our fire the talk turned to the Apaches. What if they come after us? Arthur Ripley claims to have some experience as a soldier fighting Indians. He assures us that we'll be okay if we don't raise a lot of dust and keep off the skylines. He says we will need to start making night camp a little early so we can let our night fire die down before dark. That way the Apaches won't see it and come after us.

In this discussion, I glanced over at Alito from time to time. He seemed not too interested in what was being said, but I don't think he missed anything. At one point, he seemed to almost smile, but that may have been just the way the fire played across his features.

I don't know why, but I don't trust him.

10

Breakfast the next morning was surprisingly good. Bishop wasn't sure what he expected, but the food tasted every bit as good as what Angelina served him back in her grandfather's café in Santa Fe. But he wasn't about to tell her that.

After eating, Angelina went back to their room to get something she forgot. Bishop enjoyed another cup of coffee and gazed out of the windows of the restaurant.

Across the street he noticed a mouse-colored mustang with one white stocking tied in front of what passed for a general store. Its sort of unusual coloring drew his eye. As he looked at it, A big man walked out of the store and to the horse.

At first, Bishop couldn't really tell much about the man

because he kept his head down so that his hat brim covered his face. But the size of the man and the way he walked seemed familiar.

He went to the mustang and put something in the saddle bags. Then he walked around behind the horse, keeping a hand on its rump, and checked the bindings on the pack horse tied next to the mustang. When he finished that, he lifted his head, glanced up and down the street, then directly across at the restaurant.

It was Daniel Upton! He stared at the restaurant window for a long moment as if deciding whether to come in or not. Or, as if giving Bishop a good look at his face.

Bishop knew he was far enough back in the restaurant that Upton couldn't possibly see him. But it was eerie how the man stared seemingly right at Bishop.

Why is Upton here? Bishop asked himself. Then he also gave an answer. *He's following us! He told me he always got what he wanted, one way or another. I wonder if that was his fire I saw the other night? And is he alone? Traveling alone through Apache country ain't a very wise thing to do. Should I do anything about him bein' here? But what could I do? There ain't a law against travelin' the same way other people are goin'.*

He decided there was little he could do about Upton other than keep an eye out for him. But he knew the man was dangerous. He remembered seeing that in Upton's eyes when they talked. It wouldn't do to underestimate him.

Bishop finished his coffee and went to their room to see if Angelina was about ready to go. When he came back downstairs a few minutes later, the mustang and the pack horse were both gone.

I'll remember that mustang if I ever see it again, he told himself.

The livery stable where they left their horses was a short walk from the hotel. Bishop had never been one who believed that any job that couldn't be done from the back of a horse was beneath him, like so many cowboys did. He'd walked for almost four years during the war and had no problems doing so whenever he needed to. He knew some cowboys who wouldn't cross the street if they couldn't mount up and ride there. Angelina didn't complain about walking, either.

They got to the livery stable just as Potts and Greer led their horses out of the barn. Cruz was already there, making sure the cinch was tight on his saddle.

Bishop didn't have to catch up Streak. As soon as the mule saw him walk up, he trotted over to the fence around the corral as if telling Bishop to get him out of the pen with all those horses. Bishop stroked Streak's neck and checked him over for any signs he'd been fighting with the horses. He found nothing, but it wouldn't have surprised him to find new scrapes or cuts on the mule's coat.

"Looks like you behaved yourself last night," he told

Streak. "Maybe you're beginnin' to learn how to get along with horses."

Streak butted him with his head as if to say, 'Stop talking and get me out of here.'

While Bishop was talking with Streak, Cruz caught up Angelina's horse and helped her get it saddled. Ten minutes later, the five of them headed out of Socorro.

They rode out of Socorro a little north of west, toward a little town called Magdalena. Potts said he remembered he and the men with him had spent a night there before.

About an hour out of Socorro, they stopped to check the lashings on the two pack horses. While they were stopped, Bishop stepped over to Potts.

"Where are we headed after we get to this town? You ain't said much about exactly where we're goin'."

"We'll stay the night close to Magdalena, then tomorrow we'll go on to a mountain south of there. I remember that's what we did."

Bishop stared at him. "South? Is that where that canyon full of gold is supposed to be?"

"It's one place." Potts busied himself with the lashings on his pack horse even though he'd just finished checking them.

"One place? You mean you ain't sure?"

Potts raised his head from looking at the lashings, stared off into the distance, then turned and met Bishop's eye. "You've got to remember I don't know ever'thing for sure. This bullet wound really has me bothered. Some things look familiar, but a lot don't. Besides, Sharpe took us on a real confusing route. I remember ever'body thinkin' that. I think he did it on purpose to keep us confused as to where we were goin' to find that gold. I really think his plan was to keep us from knowin' exactly which mountain we were on when we found any gold. I always thought him and whoever supplied the money for ever'thing counted on hidin' the gold we found, then comin' back for it later. I don't think he ever was plannin' to split any of the gold with us. We were there because he needed guns in case of the Apaches findin' us."

"So you don't really know where we're goin'." Bishop couldn't say he was really surprised. Even though he thought at first that Potts was lying about not remembering a lot about that expedition, maybe the man was right. He still would wait and see.

"I'm pretty sure I can recognize landmarks when I see 'em," Potts said. "And I'm hopin' that diary will have some clues in it, too. You gotta remember, none of us got to see that map Sharpe had."

"You just be sure to tell me when you see any of those landmarks you might remember. Maybe I'll remember not to shoot you before this trip is over." Bishop stomped away from the man before he gave in to his thoughts of strangling Potts.

As they rode on toward Magdalena, Bishop spotted

tracks several times. All of them looked like they were tracks of shod horses, which he took as a good sign. He pulled up beside Cruz at one point and mentioned the tracks.

"Yeah," Cruz replied. "I've seen 'em, too. They're all shod horses near as I can tell. I've heard there some miners out in the hills and mountains around here. There's also some sheep ranches a little farther north. Could be those tracks were made by some of those fellers."

They got into Magdalena when the sun was more than halfway down the western side of the sky. The little town was smaller than Socorro. A tiny sign tacked onto a post just as they rode into town showed a population of 300. As they rode down what passed for a main street, Bishop thought that number was probably high.

Nothing much stirred in Magdalena other than the wind that blew little clouds of dust down the street. Only a couple of horses were tied at hitch rails along the short street. Both of them dozed on three legs.

"A real busy place, ain't it?" Cruz said as they pulled to a stop in front of a cantina.

"Makes you wonder where they got that number of 300 people who live here," Bishop replied as he dismounted and glanced up and down the street.

There were hardly any more people inside the cantina than were visible on the street outside. A couple of men who looked like miners to Bishop leaned against a bar that seemed to sway a little as they straightened up when Angelina walked in.

"Can we get somethin' to eat?" Potts asked the man behind the bar. "And some beer?"

The man nodded and stepped through a door at the end of the bar. The five of them sat at a larger table.

After getting their eyes full of Angelina, the two miners at the bar went back to talking. "I tell you, I thought them 'Paches had me this time," one of them said. "I couldn't see 'em, but I knowed they was there all the same."

"Where were you this time?" the other one asked.

"I've been on South Baldy and Withington the last couple of months."

Bishop got up and walked over to the bar. "I heard you fellers talkin' about the Apaches in the mountains around here," he said to the miners. "They give you a hard time out there?" He got the bartender's attention and pointed at the empty mugs of the miners. The bartender refilled the mugs.

"Yeah," the miner who'd been talking the most said. "I thought for sure they had my scalp this time. You-all plannin' to head out into the mountains?"

"Thought we might. I've never been to this part of the Territory before."

The miner swigged his beer. "Don't know that I'd go back myself. Prob'ly not a good idea for anybody to now.

Especially with a good-lookin' woman along. You lookin' for gold?"

Bishop allowed a grin to show. "I'm not a miner. Wouldn't know the first thing about findin' gold. We're lookin' for a man who might've got lost out on one of these mountains. Name's Ernest Thompkins. He came out here a few weeks ago with some other men who were lookin' for gold."

The other miner nodded. "Prob'ly tryin' to find that Lost Adams Diggin's. People been tryin' to find that for a long time."

"Don't think nobody ever will," the other miner said. "And if they did, the 'Paches would prob'ly kill 'em before they could get any of it out. Most likely, that's what happened to this feller you're lookin' for."

"Could be," Bishop agreed. "But his wife wants to know if he's dead or lost out here somewhere. I told her I'd come and look for him."

"You'd be better off just stayin' here for a while, then goin' back and tellin' her he's dead. You wouldn't be tellin' no lie."

The man returned from wherever he went to get them something to eat and set it on their table. Bishop nodded to the miners, tossed a couple of silver dollars onto the bar, and said, "Use that to buy some more beers. I appreciate your advice."

The miners nodded their thanks, and Bishop went back to the table.

"Learn anything?" Angelina asked.

"Just that the Apaches don't like people out on those mountains. But I think we already knew that."

They ate, then rode out of town to a small hill where they made camp. Cruz and Bishop went out with the animals to let them graze on the small patches of grass. Cruz looked out toward the trail from Socorro to Magdalena.

"Bishop, there's dust behind us on the trail. Wonder who'd be travelin' to Magdalena other than us?"

"I don't know why you sound a little surprised, Cruz. After all, Magdalena has so many attractions for visitors these days." He paused, looking out at the dust. "There's that feller Upton I told you about. I saw him again when we left Socorro. He had a packhorse with him."

"You think he's follerin' us?"

"Could be. He's the kind who doesn't want to lose. I figger he'd foller us and wait to see if he can get his hands on that diary. That reminds me, I ain't sure about Potts, neither. I don't think he knows where they went when he came out here with Thompkins and those other men. He as much as told me that. I think he's waitin' to see what that diary says about where they went."

"So we're just sort of ridin' around, hopin' to find somethin' that tells us where Thompkins' body is, all the while tryin' to stay away from the Apaches."

"That about sums it up. It sounds like you don't think there's a chance for Thompkins to be alive."

"I don't. And I don't think you do, either."

"Yeah. I just hope somebody buried him, and those Apaches didn't kill him and leave him out for the coyotes."

11

When camp was set up and after they'd eaten their supper, Bishop brought out the diary again. He sat near the fire and squinted as he tried to read from it again. Carefully, he pulled the next few pages apart. He saw that the next entry was a couple of days after the last one.

We've covered quite a bit of ground over the last few days. After spending a night at a little town called Magdalena, Sharpe led us south toward a tall mountain he called South Baldy. He said it was the highest mountain in this part of New Mexico Territory. He continues to refer to the map he carries, but talks a lot to Alito, too. I don't know which he depends on more to get us to our goal. This South Baldy we're near looks like a loaf of bread laid out on the ground. I'm sure it will look different when we get closer. Sharpe says this is a good sign because the mountain we're looking for looks like that from a distance.

There is more irritation among the men with Charlie over the fact that Sharpe still refuses to let any of us look at the map. The others grumble a lot when he's not around. I don't know that looking at the map would do any of us much good, but the others can't seem to let it go.

I don't know that coming along on this expedition was such a good idea after all. I don't really trust the other men with Charlie. Maybe that's just because I don't know any of them very well.

Dawson, the store owner, complains a lot about the conditions we have to live under. Like I wrote before, he hasn't been out in the wilderness very much. Dixon is a very quiet man, but his eyes don't miss much. I've noticed that he watches Sharpe closely, especially when he has that map out.

Ripley brought a bottle of whiskey out tonight. Everyone seemed to think that was a good thing. All of the others shared it with him. Only me and Alito didn't drink. When I brought up that it might not be a good idea to drink when we needed to stay alert for Apaches, Ripley scoffed and said we could let Alito stand watch for us.

For some reason, maybe because I don't trust the half-Apache, that sent a shiver down my back. I surely do miss Lottie. I'm beginning to wish I hadn't come on this blasted trip. I don't know what I would've done to make things okay for us, but

I could've found some kind of work in Albuquerque. I know I could have.

But I'm here now. No need to turn back. But I can't help the feeling that this was a mistake.

Bishop laid the diary aside. From what he read, no one had any good idea where they were going. Even with he map, they were simply going from one mountain to another, hoping to find the right one. That explained some of the reason Potts didn't seem to know exactly where they needed to go now. It would've been good if the man knew the last place they were and could go right back there. But it looked like his head wound had erased that memory. If he was being truthful. For some reason, Bishop didn't think Potts was being completely truthful. He thought it was very likely he could go right to the last place that expedition went to. Unless he had reason not to.

12

They sat around the fire the next morning following breakfast talking about where they needed to go next. Bishop looked over at Potts.

"Where did you go after your group left Magdalena? Does anything look familiar around here?"

Potts couldn't meet his eye for several seconds. Then he glanced up at Bishop, then out toward South Baldy Mountain.

"I, I think we went down to that mountain."

"You think?" Bishop's voice rose a little, showing his disbelief.

"It, it looks like the mountain we climbed."

"Looks like it, or is it? Which is it?"

"It, it's the one we went to after we left Magdalena. I'm sure of it."

Bishop stood, tossed the dregs of his coffee out into the fire. "Let's get packed up and get started then."

From a distance, South Baldy Mountain looked like what Thompkins said. A loaf of bread lying on the table. But the closer they got to it, the more the peaks and valleys of the long mountain stood out.

Bishop didn't know what he expected, but the reality wasn't it. He tried to catch Potts' eye several times as they rode closer, but the other man wouldn't even look in his direction.

Finally, they got to the foothills surrounding the mountain and stopped to let the horses rest and to get something to eat. Bishop walked up to Potts as the latter was loosening the cinch on his saddle.

"This ain't the mountain you thought it was, is it?"

Potts sighed deeply. "No, it ain't. I was sure back there in Magdalena. Now, I'm not sure at all. I remember we rode across a big flat area at night. That's all, I swear."

Bishop nodded. "Well, you'll be glad to know the diary said something about comin' here, too. So we're follerin' just about the same route that you did six weeks ago." He turned on his heel and walked away from Potts. Back at the fire Cruz built so they could have coffee, he told the others.

"This ain't the mountain where that gold was supposed to be, but it is one that other expedition came to. I think we'll search around and see what's here before goin' on to somewhere else."

As they were packing up and getting ready to head out again, Angelina came up to him. "So Potts is not as good a guide as he thought he would be?"

Bishop finished tightening the cinch on his saddle, then glanced over at Potts before answering her. "I think Potts ain't tellin' all he knows. He might not really be sure about where they went, but there's somethin' that he's keepin' real close. I don't know what it is yet, but I think it might have somethin' to do with that gold. Or with Thompkins and what happened to him."

"Do you think he knows what happened to Mr. Thompkins?"

"Could be. I just ain't sure. But I know there's somethin' he ain't tellin'."

As they climbed the foothills surrounding South Baldy Mountain, they began seeing more tracks of shod horses. Not a lot of them, but enough to show people had been around the mountain.

"Those tracks aren't that old," Cruz remarked when they stopped at a place where they spotted tracks. "Prob'ly a few days old. They're headed in the same direction we're goin'."

"What do you think?" Bishop asked. "Miners, maybe?"

"Could be. Looks like two horses so it could be a miner and a pack horse."

"I gotta say, he's a lot braver than me comin' out here alone with Apaches around."

Cruz shook his head. "I don't know that I'd say he was brave. More like he got gold fever and wasn't goin' to let anything, not even Apaches, get in his way. The lure of gold can be deadly."

They rode on farther up the mountain and began making their way around it, looking for sign that would shake something loose in Potts' memory. Several times they came across the same set of tracks they saw before. Cruz remembered a chip on the edge of one of the shoes and could tell from that they were made by the same rider.

Rounding a rock formation later in the day, they came to a narrow bench along the side of the mountain. Cruz pulled to a stop a little distance onto the bench.

"What is it?" Bishop asked when he came up beside his partner.

"More tracks. That miner is in trouble." Cruz dismounted as the others gathered around. Kneeling down on the ground he showed them what he meant. "You can see here the tracks show that miner ridin' along this bench. Then over here," he pointed to the edge of the bare ground where he saw the tracks. "These are unshod horse tracks."

"Apaches?" Greer asked.

"Yep. That's my guess. And I think the Apaches came through after that miner did, so they found his tracks."

"And he ain't makin' much of an attempt at hidin' his tracks," Bishop added. "So they'll find him."

"They sure will, or prob'ly already have by now. These

tracks are only a few days old. We need to keep a sharp eye out."

No more than a half mile farther, Bishop rode in the lead of the group when he saw Streak's head come up. The mule looked off to the left of the tiny trail they followed. Streak huffed a big breath through his nose.

Bishop stopped and waved for the others to come up to him. "Streak has smelled somethin' over that way," he said, nodding off to the left.

Cruz followed Bishop's eyes and saw a small grove of mesquite trees about fifty yards from the trail. The trees sat at the edge of a clearing on the side of the mountain.

"You think it might be that miner?" he asked.

"Might be. Why don't we go take a look?" Bishop turned to Angelina and the other men. "Y'all stay here. If it's that miner, Angelina, you don't want to see it. You two keep an eye out. We'll be back in a few minutes."

He and Cruz started toward the trees, spread out a little. Both of them pulled their pistols from the holsters and kept them ready. Chances were, the Apaches were long gone, but it never hurt to be ready.

At the edge of the trees, they stopped as if both had the same thought at the same time. Listening, nothing came to their ears. With a glance at each other, they nudged their animals and walked them on into the trees. A short distance into the trees, the smell of smoke became stronger, along with another smell they both recognized.

In the middle of the little grove of mesquite trees they saw the body. The man had been stripped completely naked, so his white body showed up clearly through the trees. Even from a distance, they could tell he'd been tied spreadeagled and tortured severely.

After taking a minute to listen again, and again hearing nothing, they rode on up to the body. The man's arms and legs had been spread wide and tied to trees close by. His head lay forward, the chin touching his chest. Cruz tied his horse several feet away because the animal was spooked by the smell of the blood that covered most of the man's body. Streak didn't seem to react, but Bishop tied him away from the body anyway.

At the body, Cruz lifted the man's head and saw the Apaches had cut off his eyelids to make sure he watched what they did to him. Clearly, the man suffered. He gently lowered the head again.

The man's upper body was crisscrossed with shallow cuts just deep enough to cause pain and bring blood. A lot of blood. When they examined the lower body, it looked like the Apaches had also made several cuts on the bottoms of the man's feet. It was hard to tell because they had also built fires under each foot as well as high up between the man's legs. Finally, at some point the Apaches had cut the man's throat.

They stepped back from the body and gazed down at it

for a minute. Then Bishop asked, "What do you think we should do?"

"We could bury him, but that would tell the Apaches that we're in the neighborhood for sure." Cruz paused, thinking about what to say next. "It's not what we really want to do, but I think we should leave him here."

Bishop nodded. "Yeah, that's what I was thinkin', too. He ain't goin' to mind." He looked around the small area. Saw the man's clothes and boots lying scattered in the trees. "Wonder what they did with his horses and stuff?"

"Took 'em off when they left. Prob'ly throw stuff away when they get a chance. Keep the horses and use 'em. Or eat 'em."

There was nothing more to be said then. Bishop and Cruz mounted up and rode back out to the others.

"Was it that miner?" Potts asked before any of the others.

"Yeah," Bishop said. "It was pretty bad. The Apaches have always been good at makin' people hurt a lot when they catch 'em."

They rode on, all of them being much more watchful now. With Apaches in the area, that was the best any of them could do. The afternoon wore on with no sign of Indians or any other miners.

When the sun was more than halfway down the western sky, they stopped in a small grove of trees to let the horses rest. Bishop rode over to where Potts was sipping from his canteen.

"You seen anything that jogs your memory?"

"I was just lookin' out that way." He pointed to the southwest where the vague blue shape of another mountain lay on the horizon. Its shape was like a long loaf of bread. "That mountain looks familiar. And there's a flat prairie between here and there. I'm sure we went there. I remember crossin' a wide-open spot."

"You sure?" When Potts nodded, Bishop said, "All right. We'll head over there in the mornin'. Right now, we need to get off this mountain and find a place to camp for the night."

A few minutes later, they started off again. This time, Cruz led the way. They crossed a stream that tumbled down the mountain, across the trail, and over a tiny waterfall to splash on the rocks down below.

Only a little distance farther, Cruz pulled to a stop and examined the ground. Bishop rode up beside him.

"Find somethin'?"

Cruz pointed to the ground. "More unshod horse tracks. Looks like four or five of 'em came down this trail today. They're headed the same way we're goin'."

"Okay. Be sure to keep a sharp eye out. We don't want to run up on these Apaches."

Half a mile later, the little group made their way down a steep stretch of the trail and around a bend at the bottom of the steep part. Over to their right, a small canyon cut into the side of the mountain. Cruz would've led them right on past it if he hadn't been watching for tracks.

As it was, the tracks he found turned off the trail and headed right into the canyon. He slowed, then stopped and motioned for the others to catch up to him.

When everyone was there, he said quietly, "The tracks of those unshod horses go right into this canyon. I don't see any tracks comin' out, but the canyon might cut right on through this mountain and be open at the other end. In any case, I'm goin' to ride in there a little way and see what there is in there."

"Let's all go," Bishop suggested. "If the canyon does cut all the way through, it might be a shortcut to gettin' off this mountain."

They rode into the canyon slowly, with rifles and pistols drawn, ready to use. About halfway through, they came upon a burned-out fire in a ring of rocks. Cruz dismounted and stepped over to the ashes.

"Still just a little warm," he said after putting his hand on the ashes. "I'd say this fire was made this mornin'. Apaches, for sure."

Bishop took a moment to gaze around at the steep sides of the canyon. Too steep for any animals to climb. A man might get to the top, but it would be a hard climb. But if those Apaches were as familiar with the mountain as he figured they were, they would know a way around so that they could get on top of the canyon. Once they were up there, they could cut to pieces anybody down on the floor of the canyon.

Like them.

"We need to get on out of this canyon. I don't know where those Apaches went, but I don't want to be down in here if they get up there."

That seemed to get all of them thinking about what Bishop said. It only took them a few minutes to get to the end of the canyon. Once there, they saw another grove of trees a short distance away from the mountain. Cruz led them there.

No MORE THAN a mile behind them, Daniel Upton stopped. He'd been following the tracks of Bishop and those with him all day. He looked at the tracks headed into the short canyon.

I don't like the looks of that canyon, but that's where Bishop went. I think it prob'ly cuts through the mountain and they're goin' to foller it and make camp somewhere. Maybe I can find where they are and what they're goin' to do next. I don't know why they didn't stay here longer unless this ain't the right mountain.

Cautiously, he rode on into the canyon, his pistol in his hand. He found the same fire ring used by the Apaches and rode on past it. At the end of the canyon, he stopped and looked out at the small grove of trees ahead. In the slanting rays of the sun, he saw Bishop's tracks lead on to that grove.

Looks like this is where I camp tonight. Wonder if they're headed out to another mountain? That would explain why they didn't stay longer. Oh well, I'll let them do all the work of leadin' me to that gold, then take it away from 'em. Either that, or get that diary and find it myself.

He reined his horse over to a small boulder and started silently making his camp.

13

The grove of mesquite trees Bishop and the others saw from the mouth of the canyon was about two miles out from the mountain itself. They rode down the side of the mountain following a game trail, then rode across a short open space to get to the trees.

That open space they had to cross bothered Bishop a lot. If those Apaches had a lookout posted anywhere on the side of South Baldy Mountain, he would've seen them crossing. They would know exactly where to come and attack them.

Once inside the trees, he told the others, "Let's camp here for the night. We can have a fire for cooking, then let it burn out before full dark. If there's no water in these trees, we better go easy on what we've got. I don't know where we can fill our canteens next."

Inside the trees, they found a stream that flowed down from the higher levels of South Baldy, then went underground for little way, and bubbled up to form a pool and a stream that flowed away from the mountain. Cruz and Angelina set to work getting them something to eat.

As they ate, Bishop underlined the danger they were in. "We don't know where those Apaches went from that canyon, but they may have crossed this open prairie between us and that mountain out there south of us. Or they may have just circled around the mountain behind us. I think we need to take turns bein' on guard duty tonight. The four of us men can take two hours each." Angelina started to say something, but Bishop held up a hand to stop her. "I'm sure we'll want to keep up guard duty at night from here on. You'll get the chance beginnin' tomorrow night. I'll take the last shift this time. If those Apaches are goin' to hit us, most likely that's the time they'll do it. Anybody have a better idea?" No one spoke up in the next couple of minutes. "Okay. Let the fire die down before dark. Ever'body prob'ly needs to go ahead and get some sleep."

While everyone was getting settled and beginning to roll up in their blankets, Bishop pulled out the diary. The pages were not as easy to pull apart now without tearing them. But he managed to get two separated and began to read.

There is more irritation and complaining tonight. We have searched South Baldy Mountain and found nothing that would come close to being a canyon filled with gold. Once we made camp, the others asked Ripley to bring out the whiskey he has left and pass it around. He refused in no uncertain terms. He accused someone (he never named this person) of drinking more than his share. Of course, that led to a lot of denials and finger-pointing. Once again, only Alito and I refrained from joining in the argument. It did seem like Alito was pleased to see the men fussing and fuming like they did.

I am more and more concerned about that map Sharpe told us showed just where to go. We're just riding from one mountain to another.

There was a break in the diary then. It picked up a day later.

Fortunately, nothing came of the arguing last night. But today was different. We had not been on the way for an hour before Alito made us aware of Apaches no more than a half-mile ahead of us. He led us to a bench on the side of South Baldy where we hid for the rest of today. Our thinking was not to leave tracks for the Apaches to find. At one point, the Indians came near enough to our hiding place for me to see them clearly. I have not seen better examples of fighting men anywhere. Fierce is too slight a word to describe them.

Two good things came from our predicament today. First, no one argued about not having Ripley's whiskey shared tonight around the fire. The presence of Apaches so close by seems to have blended us into a group of one mind. That mind being to survive. Second, while we were trapped on the bench, Dixon began quietly chipping at the side of the mountain that had been exposed to the weather. He found some small nuggets of gold right there on the bench where we hid. Needless to say, that discovery lifted our spirits tremendously.

Perhaps I will be able to return to Lottie with something good to show for this time away from her. I certainly hope so. I miss her a great deal.

It is my understanding from what Sharpe said after consulting his map around the fire that we are heading to another mountain a little south of here. That mountain is called Mount Withington. We must ride across an open stretch of prairie, so we will be easily seen if the Apaches so desire.

That day's diary entry ended there. As Bishop put the diary back in his saddle bag next to his bedroll, he felt pleased to know they were still on the trail of that first expedition.

14

Clouds and no wind greeted them the next morning. The clouds were so low it looked like they skimmed along the tops of the mountains. No one seemed very talkative at breakfast, everyone content just to get their food and find a place to sit and eat it. It was like the weather pressed down on them and pushed them each into their own world.

Bishop thought about the crossing of the open prairie they faced that day. Part of the problem with the crossing was whether to ride fast and get across quickly or take it slower and not raise so much dust.

Riding fast would bring on the problem of dust. And with little wind so far, that dust would hang in the air and be visible for a long time. Getting across the open space quickly would give them time to find a good position to make a stand if the Apaches saw them. But Bishop wanted to make the crossing and not have to stand and fight anywhere.

Making the crossing slower and raising less dust would be good. But it would put them out in the open longer and make them vulnerable to being seen for a longer time. And if the Apaches saw them they would have less time to find a good spot to defend.

When everyone finished breakfast and had gotten ready to go, he told them, "We'll ride across this open area slowly. I know that means we'll be in the open longer, but we won't raise as much dust. With no wind blowing, dust would hang in the air and make it more likely the Apaches would see it. I think this will be the better way."

"Why don't we just ride across real fast, get to that other mountain, and fort up?" Potts asked. "No need to stay out in the open for so long."

"I thought about that," Bishop replied. "And I still think goin' slow is the best way."

"Who made you the boss of this here search?" Greer asked, his face scrunched up as if daring Bishop to do something.

"If you don't like me makin' the decisions, you're welcome to ride on by yourself." Bishop had no patience with the man. He felt toward Greer like he did toward Potts. There was something about the man he just didn't like. Maybe it was because he was a friend of Potts' and Bishop didn't know he was coming along with them. Or maybe it was something else. In either case, he didn't want to argue.

When Greer saw that Bishop wasn't going to back down from his decision, he huffed through his nose and went back to getting ready to ride.

They crossed the open space with no trouble. It was about two miles across. This time, the mountain continued to look more rounded the closer they got, unlike South Baldy. That was one thing Potts remembered about the mountain where they may have found the gold. It looked like a loaf of bread even up close.

Once they were at the base of Mount Withington, Bishop stopped them in a small nest of rocks to rest the horses and see if they could tell whether the Apaches might have seen them and decided to come after them.

None of them had seen anything after several minutes, so they started to head on up the mountain. But Cruz gazed out across the open area one last time.

"Bishop," he called quietly. "There's some dust out there."

The others turned to look out across the prairie. A small plume of dust hung in the still air back almost all the way to South Baldy Mountain.

After watching it for a moment, Bishop said, "If it's Apaches, they'll likely find our tracks. If it's not, whoever it is will likely bring the Apaches with him once they see that dust. We prob'ly should get on up the mountain."

The lower part of Mount Withington was covered in trees and was home to all kinds of animals. Several times, they came upon deer they spooked out of bedding areas. Those deer would bound through the trees for a way, then stop and stare at them as they rode.

"We could get some fresh meat here," Bishop told Cruz in a low voice. "But any shots would let the Apaches know right where we are."

"Maybe I could fix up a bow and some arrows," Cruz replied. "Wouldn't make that much noise to kill a deer with an arrow."

"That's somethin' to think about for sure. We've got plenty of supplies right now, but if we start to run low, you might consider that."

Cruz nodded. "I'll start lookin' around for the right materials."

They wound around the mountain following the plentiful game trails for another three miles or so. The trails became steeper, and their horses began working harder.

At a place where a wide stream cut across the trail they followed, they stopped to let the horses drink and rest. Angelina climbed down to splash some water on her face. When she knelt down at the edge of the stream, she hesitated as something caught her eye.

"John, come take a look at this," she called softly.

"What is it?" he asked when he came to her side.

She pointed to a track in the mud no more than a foot

from where she knelt. He saw the characteristic track of a mountain lion. The foot pad and four toe prints showed clearly in the mud.

Cruz came over to them. "That is a big cougar," he said, kneeling down and placing his hand on the track. The track was wider than his hand and almost as long.

"We should expect there to be mountain lions out here after all these deer," Bishop said. "We'll have to keep an eye on the horses at night. A lion that big could take one of them down."

They rode on for the rest of that day, climbing higher on the mountain, but not seeing any sign of people being there. When the sun was well on its way toward the western horizon, Cruz rode ahead to find a place to make their night camp. He came back a few minutes later and led them to a sheltered cut in the side of the mountain. There was water there from a spring that trickled out of the side of the mountain. It made a small pool that would provide plenty of water for the animals. It also formed a small stream that flowed along the contour of the mountain for a hundred yards before plunging over the side of the mountain in a small waterfall.

After they saw to their animals, Angelina told Bishop, "I am going downstream a little way to wash up. I feel like I have so much dirt on me you might not want me to sleep beside you again."

Bishop took her in his arms. "I'll always want you to

sleep beside me, no matter how much dirt you've got on you. But I'll go with you if you want."

She hugged him tightly. "No, my husband. I am thinking if we go together, the temptation may be too much to do something other than get clean. I will be all right. I have my pistol."

He grinned. "Already you can read my mind. Okay, but you call out if anything happens. I'll be there fast."

She gathered up what she needed and walked down the stream until she found a spot behind a screen of saplings and bushes. On the rocks there, she partially undressed and washed herself with the clear, cold water from the mountain. After she finished and dressed again, a tiny noise from the screen of saplings got her attention. As she turned, she brought up the Colt Pocket Revolver and pulled the hammer back.

Greer, the half-breed, stood there, a sly grin on his face.

"You do realize it is not polite to sneak up on a woman while she is bathing?" Angelina kept the pistol pointed right at Greer's midsection.

"I have always wanted a Spanish woman," Greer said, his eyes roving over Angelina's body.

She ignored the slimy feeling she got just from the man's gaze touching her. "If you try anything with me, I will shoot you. Do not think I will not."

"Oh, I don't think you will shoot me. If you do, you will

give away where we are to the Apaches," he replied with a grin.

"Well, that would not be any concern of yours, because you would be dead. I hit what I aim at. Remember that time back in Socorro?"

Greer shrugged. "Maybe I'm willing to try anyway."

"If you do try something with me, I might not shoot you, but my husband will cut your throat."

The half-breed scoffed. "Maybe I'll kill Bishop, then take you."

Even though the thought of such a thing drove a stake into Angelina's heart, she didn't show anything. "If you were to take me, I would kill you in your sleep the first chance I got."

"You are a fiery one," Greer said with another grin. "I like that. All right, I'll leave you alone for now. But keep in mind what I said. Maybe the Apaches will kill Bishop, and you will have to come to me to protect you." He stepped backward into the saplings. "Until then, you be sure to sleep well."

Angelina made sure he was gone, then gathered up her things, and walked back to the fire. She decided she wouldn't say anything to Bishop about Greer. They didn't need to be one man short with the Apaches around.

She didn't see Cruz standing beside a large boulder. He had heard and seen everything that went on between her and Greer. He'd seen the half-breed follow Angelina when she went to clean herself up and followed them. It would've been easy for him to sneak up on Greer and put a knife in his kidney.

I'm goin' to have to talk to that feller, he told himself. *Maybe even kill him sometime.*

15

Neither Angelina nor Cruz said anything to Bishop about Greer talking with her. Cruz came back to the fire after Angelina, so she didn't even know he'd seen the encounter.

While Cruz and Angelina put together something for supper, Bishop walked out to a spot where he could see a part of the mountain behind them. Dusk was gathering in the canyons on the sides of the mountain away from the sun, getting ready to flow across the ground as the sun slipped away. He stepped behind a cedar tree that had its top curled over by the almost constant winds. It was just tall enough to allow him to see over it, but be hard to see from any distance.

He gazed out across the short open prairie they had crossed earlier and where they'd seen the dust behind them. There was no dust visible in the gathering gloom of dusk. But he caught the wink of light from a small fire down below them on the side of the mountain. From what he could tell, it must've been a couple of miles away, at least. Whoever it was either didn't know or didn't care about the Apaches.

Bishop watched the small fire for a few more minutes, then turned and walked back to their fire. While he waited for supper to be ready, he pulled out the diary and slowly worked at the next couple of pages to get them loose. By the time it was time to eat, he had two pages separated. He laid the diary down on his saddle and got his food.

Once everyone had eaten and everything was ready for breakfast, Bishop picked up the diary, held it close to the light from the fire, and began reading.

Tragedy has struck our group. Dawson McAlister, the store owner and probably least prepared of our group, is dead. He was bitten in the neck by a rattlesnake.

Until tonight, none of us had even seen any snakes on this expedition. In fact, Sharpe had said only yesterday that it was still too cold for the snakes to come out of hibernation.

Apparently, McAlister unrolled his blankets right next to a rock where the snake was coiled. I don't know how he could have missed seeing it. Or hearing it rattle. In any case, he said he was exhausted and decided to lay down until supper was ready. In no time after he stretched out on his blankets he gave out with a bloodcurdling scream and jumped up from the ground, one hand on his neck. He took only a few steps and fell to the ground. He was dead before any of us could get to him.

Alito found the snake and killed it. He tossed it into the brush.

For a few minutes, no one seemed to know what to do. Then, Arthur Ripley said we might as well bury him. There was nothing else to do, but the way he said it, and the way the others just got busy and carried out the gruesome task made me feel strange, like I should've done or said something. But I don't know what.

It was almost like everyone expected him to be the first to die, if anyone did.

The death kept talk around the fire that night to a minimum. No one talked about gold or how to split what we find five ways instead of six. That was good, I think. But also no one said anything about what a great friend McAlister was or how much they'd miss him or anything like that. Not knowing the man other than the few days we'd been together, I didn't know what to say.

I'm feeling more than ever that this expedition was a bad idea. I wish Charlie had never asked me to come along. Most of all, I miss Lottie.

There's a heavy feeling in my chest and not one having to do with McAlister's death. If he'd been a friend, I might think this feeling is because of him no longer being with us. But this is different. I'm starting to think I might not get back home.

Every time I look at Alito, he seems to be staring at one or the other of us. I wonder what's behind those flat black eyes?

BEHIND THEM AND below them on Mount Witherington, Upton sat beside his own fire. He thought about Apaches possibly seeing it, but dismissed that idea since he'd seen no tracks or any other sign of Indians.

Crossing the flat plain, he'd decided to ride fast and not stay out in the open any longer than necessary. But once he got a little over halfway across, he happened to think about the dust he was raising. Thinking it was too late to do anything about it, he just kept on going.

Some, maybe most, of his decision was guided by wanting to get his hands on that diary and find out where that canyon filled with gold was. Ever since the first expedition came up with no gold, he became obsessed with finding it himself.

He needed that gold.

16

After a night plagued with dreams he couldn't remember other than knowing they were disturbing, Bishop awoke to clear skies and cooler temperatures. From his blankets, he gazed up at the carpet of stars flung across the remaining dark sky. As he watched, a shooting star blazed a bright trail across the other stars, ending in a soundless explosion far to the west.

All my life I've heard seeing a shooting star meant somebody was going to die, he told himself. *But that's just a folk tale. I hope.*

Easing out of his blankets, he tucked them around Angelina. All he could see of her was her black hair sticking out from under her blankets.

After taking care of his morning needs, he returned to the fire ring and gently moved the blackened sticks around until he found a red wink of a live coal. He laid some shavings from a mesquite branch over the coal and blew softly. In a minute, a tiny tendril of smoke rose from the shavings. A few more breaths brought a tiny blaze. By laying progressively larger sticks and then branches on the growing fire, Bishop soon had flames that brought some warmth to his chilled hands. He set the water-filled coffee pot close to the flames.

In only a few more minutes, the others were awake and beginning to gather around the fire. Angelina began putting together their breakfast.

Half an hour later, they were finished with breakfast and drinking the last of their morning coffee. Bishop tossed the dregs of his coffee onto the fire.

"I think we should split up today and take a look around the mountain." He let his gaze roam from one face to the other.

"Is it smart to split up like that?" Potts asked. "What about the Apaches?"

"We haven't seen any sign of Apaches on this mountain. Not even any old tracks. I think if we're very careful and keep a sharp eye out, we should be okay. If any of us run into trouble with Apaches, the others will hear the gun shots and run to help. We can cover the mountain faster that way."

No one had any other ideas, so they got everything cleaned up and split into two groups. Potts and Greer rode around the mountain one way while Bishop, Angelina, and Cruz rode the opposite way. They planned to meet up again in the middle of the afternoon somewhere close to the camp they were leaving.

Bishop, Angelina, and Cruz found nothing that indicated anyone had been on the part of the mountain they searched. If there were tracks, they were so old as to be little more than indentations in the soft ground.

Mid-day came and went with nothing of interest found. They found a tiny stream flowing down the mountain and stopped to let their horses rest. Lunch was jerky and water from the stream.

"I'm beginnin' to think this ain't the mountain where that gold is supposed to be," Cruz said as he sat back against a boulder, his eyes almost closed. "We ain't seen a canyon, much less one with gold layin' around on the ground."

Angelina sat back against another boulder fanning herself with her hat. "I thought it was going to be cool all day, but the sun is making everything warm. We have not seen any old camps or even recent tracks. I agree with Cruz. This can not be the mountain of gold."

Bishop squinted up at the sun's position. "It's just past the middle of the day. We'll ride on a little way farther, then make our way back to the meetin' place."

They got to their feet and caught up their animals. Each of them made sure they tightened their cinches on the saddles. It wouldn't do for a saddle to slip and cause one of them to fall off their ride. If something like that happened at the wrong time or in the wrong place, whoever fell could be seriously hurt. And a serious injury out where they were could be fatal.

They rode for another hour, finding nothing. Bishop was about to suggest they turn around and go back to meet Potts and Greer when Cruz spotted something.

"Look ahead of us, Bishop. That looks like somebody pulled those downed trees around to make a fort."

Bishop saw what Cruz pointed out to him. He knew there were few times in nature that something ended up being in a mostly straight line like what he looked at. It might be nothing but blowdowns from a long-ago storm, but it was something that needed to be examined.

They rode up to the trees and found bullet scars on them. Also, rocks had been pulled up to close gaps along the breastworks. Those rocks had bullet scars, too.

"Somebody had a fight here," Cruz said. "Look, there are spent cartridges on the ground."

They dismounted and handed their reins to Angelina. It was clear that there were several people who were firing from inside the hastily build fort.

"I'll bet this is where somebody fought off Apaches," Bishop said. "And they were successful. If they weren't, there would still be some evidence of bodies here. I wonder if this was that party that Potts was part of."

"I'll ride back to the place where we're supposed to meet and bring Potts and Greer back here," Cruz said. "Will you and Angelina be all right?"

"Sure. We'll hide in here and wait for you."

It took Cruz the better part of three hours to get back with Potts and Greer. They pulled up in front of the breastworks and dismounted.

Potts walked around the area seeming to take it all in. "I remember this place. We had a fight with the Apaches here. We knew they were comin' in time to drag up these trees and rocks. None of us were hurt bad, but we killed at least a couple of the Apaches."

"You remember where you went from here?" Bishop asked.

Potts turned in a circle, taking his time to answer. "Yeah. We went off that way." He pointed to the northwest. "There's another mountain out there. We had to ride across a big open space that time. We did it at night so the Apaches wouldn't see us."

"Let's make camp on a little farther," Bishop said. "We've got an hour of light left, and I don't really want to camp where there was a fight. Besides, there's no water here."

They rode another quarter mile around the mountain, heading generally in the direction Potts remembered his party going from there. Cruz found another sheltered spot in the side of the mountain with a spring to provide water.

After taking care of Streak, Bishop walked out a little way from their camp. In the dirt of a smaller trail he saw a fresh track. It was a shod horse, and not one he'd seen before. A little farther down that trail, the same spring formed a small stream that cut across the trail. There, he found a boot print. A large boot print. One large enough to belong to Daniel Upton.

17

When he came back to their camp, Bishop didn't say anything about seeing the boot print. He got his food and sat down on his blankets, leaning against his saddle. He reached across his saddle and pulled the diary from his saddle bag.

After finishing his supper and helping with the clean-up, Bishop went back to his blankets and began working to loosen a couple more pages of Thompkins' diary. He worked gently and soon had the pages free. The writing had faded a lot, but by holding the diary close to the fire he was able to make out what Thompkins had written. It looked like a few days had passed since the last entry.

This has been a terrible few days. Two days ago, a band of Apaches got on our trail, at least according to Alito. He rode into a camp we'd made where some trees had fallen over in a past storm and said the Apaches were coming and they were close. We hurried and pulled some of the trees around to make a sort of fort. Then we waited all night.

The Apaches came at us just at first light. It was horrible! I've never been in a fight like that before. Shouting, screaming, Apaches running at us almost naked. If Alito hadn't warned us, we'd all have been killed. As it was, Sharpe and Ripley were wounded slightly. I think we must've killed two or three Apaches, but we never found any bodies. Ripley said Indians usually dragged off their dead after a fight, so it wasn't surprising we found no one.

We stayed in our 'fort' for half of the day to make sure the Apaches didn't come back. Alito went out about mid-day, then came back and said there weren't any Apaches close by.

That was the first time in a day I breathed easy.

Sharpe talked to Alito who told him we were on the wrong mountain. Apparently, the map Sharpe had wasn't as good as it was supposed to be. The rest of us had gotten about an hour's sleep while they talked. When he woke us, Sharpe told us what Alito said. He said we had to go northwest to the Datil Mountains about 40 miles away. Madre Mountain was where we had to go. Alito said that was where the canyon filled with gold could be found. Almost half of that 40 miles was across a wide open plain. We'd be completely out in the open, easy to see if any Apaches were looking. There would be no cover to speak of.

We talked about the trip a lot. None of us wanted to be out in *the open like that, but the lure of gold for the taking was strong. In the end, we decided to cross the open prairie at night.*

We rode on a few more miles and camped again. All of us were exhausted from not getting any sleep the night before the fight. Everybody turned in early.

Sometime after dark we were awakened by the sounds of a fight. Men grunting, blows landing, curses like I've never heard before. Sharpe and Dixon Howard were fighting. Once we had the two separated, Sharpe accused Howard of trying to steal the map while Sharpe was asleep. Howard didn't deny it. Instead, he admitted trying to get a look at the map since Sharpe hadn't let anyone see it.

This led to a general discussion about Sharpe needing to let the rest of us see the map. He absolutely refused. I'm not sure why; maybe he was just being stubborn. After all, the map had just been proven not to be accurate.

In any case, the argument grew so strong that Sharpe decided to camp away from the rest of us, but close by. All of us tried to persuade him that such an idea could get him killed. An Apache could sneak up on him at night and cut his throat. In spite of our pleadings, Sharpe immediately moved his blankets and other gear a little distance away. I can only hope no Apaches find him alone out there.

The entry stopped at the bottom of that page. It would take some time to work loose any more pages, and Bishop was tired. He laid the diary beside him and rolled into his blankets beside Angelina.

Later in the night, Bishop's eyes flared open. He didn't move, but listened closely to the night.

What woke me up? Something did, but I don't hear anything. As tired as I was, I thought I'd sleep through the night with no problem. So why did I wake up?

Then a tiny sound caught his attention. It was the kind of sound a boot would make when it was very carefully set down on hard ground. Was somebody moving around in the camp?

Bishop moved his head slightly so he could see a part of the camp. The fire had died down to coals, so it didn't put out much light. But it made enough to show him a darker form against the night moving at the edge of the camp. It looked like a man stepping away and into the surrounding trees. He couldn't see the form clearly enough to make out who it was.

Maybe somebody had to get up and go into the bushes, he thought. *Whoever it was should come back in a few minutes. I wish I could've seen better. Maybe I'm just gettin' spooked a little bit. This country can do that to a man. But there are Apaches around, although if that was one of them, he would've killed one or all of us. And Daniel Upton may be close by, too.*

He drifted off to sleep again, not seeing that whoever he'd seen didn't return to the camp.

After breakfast the next morning when he was getting ready to saddle Streak, Bishop noticed that his saddle bags had been searched. Whoever did it tried to put everything back like he had it, but left enough moved around that Bishop could tell.

Could whoever was up last night have looked through my saddle bags? Ever'body knows I don't have anything of value in there. The only thing that anybody could possibly want was Thompkins' diary. I'm glad I kept it under my blankets last night.

A LITTLE OVER a mile away from Bishop's camp, Upton drank some coffee and thought about the night before.

I could've had that diary if Bishop had left it in his saddle bag like I thought he might have. That was the obvious place to keep it, but it wasn't there. I don't know if maybe the woman had it, but it was too much of a risk to search her saddle bags. They were right beside her head. She might've heard and woke up. Then I would've had to do something to keep her from sounding an alarm, and that might've woke Bishop up. I'll just keep on follerin' them until I can get my hands on it. Now I know I can slip into their camp even thought they have a guard on their animals.

He finished his coffee and got ready to follow Bishop for that day.

18

Bishop decided not to say anything to the others about seeing what might've been a man the night before. After all, he could've been dreaming, no matter that he thought he was wide awake. As exhausted as he felt, he most likely was in a deep sleep and dreaming about someone being there. And he didn't really know if someone had searched his saddle bags. He might've put things back in a different way when the got the diary out the last time. To avoid making people think he was seeing things, he kept the incident quiet.

After finishing breakfast, they rode for a couple of hours finally getting completely off the mountain. At the edge of a huge flat plain, they stopped.

Potts rode up beside Bishop where they halted inside the trees. "This is a big open prairie," he said. "I remember having to cross this. Northwest is Madre Mountain. That's where the gold is supposed to be."

"Sounds like you've started rememberin' more," Bishop said, his voice flat. "Have you remembered where you got separated from Thompkins?"

"Not yet." Potts shook his head while he gazed out across the flat plain. "But it has to be over there on Madre Mountain, don't you think?"

"If that's really the last place you went when you were here. I hope you'll remember about Thompkins when we get to that other mountain."

They rode back into the trees a short distance and talked about what to do. Bishop led off.

"I think we have two choices. We can go ahead and cross in the daytime, movin' slow to keep the dust down, and hope no Apaches are lookin' out over that wide stretch of flat ground. Or, we can wait until dark and cross then. Both ways will be slow, but we'll have a better chance of not bein' seen if we go across at night."

Potts spoke up. "That's what we did when me and the other boys crossed it. Nighttime is the best."

"You remember how long it took you to cross?"

"I remember we rode all night without stoppin'. That would make it prob'ly twenty miles across."

"There will be a pretty good moon tonight," Bishop said. "It will give us pretty good light to go by. I think we should all rest today, then we'll ride across that open area tonight."

Everybody began laying out their bedrolls to try and get some sleep. No one completely unpacked so that they could get away fast if they needed to. They all remembered the Apaches were still in the area.

Cruz spread his blankets under a low-growing cedar at the edge of a small clearing. He stretched out with his hat covering his eyes, but didn't sleep. Instead, he watched from under the brim of his hat as Greer untied his bedroll, put it under his arm, and walked off a little way from the rest.

After giving the man plenty of time to get settled, Cruz glanced around at the rest of the group. All of them were laying down in the shade seemingly asleep. Slowly, he sat up and pushed the hat off his eyes. No one moved among the others. He eased to his feet, checking the entire time to make sure no one was watching. Then he started off in the direction that Greer had taken.

No one he knew was better than Cruz when it came to moving through about any kind of terrain with almost no noise. As he moved this time, he watched closely where he put his feet. There were limbs and leaves all over the ground, so it was no simple matter not to step on a limb, break it, and give himself away.

Taking his time, it took Cruz ten minutes to find Greer and sneak up almost within touching distance of him. The half-breed lay on his back, eyes closed, mouth open, a tiny bit of spit visible at the corner of his mouth.

Cruz watched Greer for a minute before stepping closer. When he stood over the sleeping Greer, he reached behind his back and pulled out a knife with an eight-inch blade that was sharp enough to cut through boot leather. Old boot leather.

After a glance around, Cruz slowly knelt beside Greer. When he got that close, he got a noseful of the man's breath. Even that didn't cause him to think twice about what he was going to do.

Carefully, he laid the blade of his knife against Greer's throat. When the cold steel touched his neck, Greer's eyes flew open.

"I wouldn't move if I was you," Cruz said in a low voice. "You might accidentally cut your own throat."

Greer's eyes grew wide and fastened onto Cruz' face. The man blinked hard a few times as if he couldn't believe what he saw.

Cruz went on in that soft, but serious voice. "I'm only goin' to tell you this one time. If you bother Angelina again, you won't have to worry about facin' Bishop. I'll come to you in the middle of the night some night and cut your throat from ear to ear. My face will be the last thing you ever see." As if to prove what he said, Cruz put just enough pressure on the knife blade to dent the skin of Greer's

throat, but not hard enough to draw blood. "Do you believe
what I'm sayin'? If you do, blink twice."

Greer blinked twice, hard.

"Good. I'm goin' to leave now. It will be best if you don't
move. If I look back and see you movin', I might think
you're goin' to try to draw that pistol and shoot me. And if I
think that, well, you know what I'll do. Keep in mind you
ain't seen me use a pistol yet, but you can't outdraw me.
Take my word for it." Cruz paused, just long enough for
Greer to understand what he said. Then he went on. "Do
you believe me? Blink twice if you do."

Once again, Greer blinked twice.

Cruz stood in one smooth, fluid motion. Returning his
knife to its sheath, he stepped backward two steps, then
turned and vanished into the trees.

19

The sun was nearly touching the mountains to the west when all of them gathered back at a small fire Cruz had built. Greer came into the camp last. He never glanced at Cruz.

"Put together something for us to eat," Bishop told Cruz and Angelina. "And make the coffee strong. We need to stay awake all night."

While they worked on the meal, Bishop walked out to the edge of the trees and gazed out across the open plain. In the distance, he spotted a small cloud of dust. Just the right size for a small band of Apaches to ride under. Fortunately, the dust seemed to be going across the plain in front of him and not coming right for them. He watched the dust until it went almost out of sight to the west. Then he walked back to the fire.

"We'll eat, then go on across as soon as it's dark enough," he told the others there.

They kept the fire they used for cooking as small as possible and used the driest wood they could find, everything they could do to keep the Apaches from spotting them. No one talked much as they ate. Greer got his food and walked a little way away from the rest. Never once did he glance toward Cruz.

After he finished eating, Bishop walked out toward the edge of the trees to gaze across the distance toward Madre Mountain. In the growing dusk, flowing out of the canyons of the mountain behind him, he couldn't really make out the mountain. As he peered that way, he saw a distant flash of lightning momentarily light the sky behind the far mountain. Listening closely, he never heard the thunder that he knew came with the lightning.

Pretty far off, he told himself. *That's good. Maybe it'll stay way off on the other side of the mountain.*

Cruz came up beside him. "See anything?"

"No. Nothing moving out there that I can see. There's a storm on the other side of that mountain where we're headed. Every once in a while I can see the lightning."

"I hope it stays way out there. We don't want to get caught in a storm out in the open. We'd be the highest things around. You know how lightning likes that."

"We'll have to keep an eye on it." Bishop raised his eyes and looked at the sky. "At least it's still clear here. And it looks like maybe it's clear all the way across." They grew quiet then, listening as much as watching for movement out on the bare plain. In another few minutes, Bishop said, "It'll be dark soon, and we can get started."

Back with the others, they helped get things ready to go. Once everything was packed, and the darkness covered the plain, Bishop told them, "We have to be as quiet as possible during this crossin'. All of you know how sound carries at night, and we have to think that there are Apaches listenin'. We'll try to keep as straight a line as we can on that mountain, but there might be times we have to ride one way or another to get around somethin'. Any time you think we're veerin' off-track, say somethin', but say it low. And if you see or hear somethin', say so. We want to get across this stretch before daylight." He met the eyes of each one in turn. Greer barely let his eyes touch Bishop's before turning away. Bishop thought about that for a second, then decided it wasn't something he wanted to follow up on just then. "All right. Mount up, and let's get goin'."

Fortunately, the ground across the bare plain was mostly sand. There were rocks here and there, some of them big enough to be seen and avoided. But Bishop knew there would others they couldn't see. He worried about the horses hitting those rocks and making enough noise to get them caught. Only a few minutes after they got started the full moon rose above the mountains east of them. It would cast enough light for them to avoid most of the smaller rocks, too. But its cold light would also make them more visible to some sharp-eyed Apache. And there were plenty of those around. He just hoped they all were gathered around a nice warm fire somewhere and getting ready to sleep.

As usual in desert and semi-desert areas, once the sun went down the air became cooler. By dawn, their jackets would feel good. In spite of the coolness of the air, Bishop felt sweat build up under his arms.

They kept their horses at a fast walk. Any faster than that, and they ran the risk of making more noise and of running into something they weren't planning on. None of them knew the plain and what kind of terrain it held. Only Potts had been across it before, and that was at night.

After an hour, Bishop stopped the little column. "We'll let the horses rest a little and listen to the night," he explained in a very low voice.

They heard little during the stop. Far off on one of the mountains, a coyote sang its mournful tune. Just before they started off again, Bishop heard the scream of a dying rabbit. *That coyote must've caught its supper,* he told himself.

At the end of the second hour of riding, they came to the first unexpected obstacle, although it was one they should have expected.

Bishop was riding along in the lead when he spotted a darker area in front of him in the dim moonlight. He pulled Streak to a stop and dismounted. Keeping hold of Streak's reins, he stepped forward to the edge of what he now recognized as an arroyo. Kneeling down at the edge, he couldn't tell how deep it was.

When he got back to the others, he told them, "There's an arroyo just ahead. I can't tell how deep it is or how wide. Stay here. I'm going to ride off to the left and see if I can find either an end to it or a place we can ride down and maybe get across it."

He climbed back onto Streak and headed off. Only about thirty yards farther he found a spot where the bank of the arroyo on their side had either caved in or washed away. From what Bishop could tell it would be an easy place for the horses to manage. He urged Streak down the incline and to the bottom of the arroyo. It was a lot deeper than he'd thought before. The bank on the other side was shorter and much less steep. He knew they could cross there.

Back at the others, he didn't say anything, just waved for them to follow him. They got across the arroyo with no problems. On the other side, Bishop got a glimpse of Madre Mountain low on the horizon when lightning flared behind it again.

Another hour passed with very little sound from the small column. Even the animals seemed to sense the need for as much quiet as possible. They made little sound and avoided hitting their hooves on rocks.

Traveling at night across unfamiliar ground while

trying not make any noise led to a lot of stress that then led to fatigue. Knowing that any sound they made could be heard by Apaches who would then rush to attack them drained every one of them.

Bishop stopped them and said quietly, "We need to let the horses rest for a bit. Go ahead and climb down, but keep the reins in your hands. You can't afford to let your horse wander off out here. We might never find it. If you have some jerky, go ahead and eat. Take care of your other needs, too."

They stayed there for about half an hour. During that time, Angelina came up to him.

"I have been watching the lightning ahead of us. Is that storm coming our way?"

"If it is, it's coming real slow," Bishop said. "I can still see stars way ahead of us. I'm hopin' it's goin' to stay behind that mountain ahead of us. Maybe it'll wait until we get to the mountain and find some shelter, then come out this way and wash out our tracks."

The rest of their trip across the plain passed uneventfully. Bishop saw clouds beginning to cover the stars the closer they got to Madre Mountain. Before they made it to the mountain, thunder rolled over them as well.

By the time they rode into the junipers and pinyons ringing the edge of the mountain, the sun was just beginning to peer over the edge of the world. A magnificent red colored the edges of the clouds that hovered over the top of the sun. Lightning flashed more frequently, so Bishop knew they had to find shelter quickly.

They followed a small game trail through the trees, hoping it would lead them to some place they could stay out of the storm. More wind pushed ahead of the storm, gradually becoming stronger.

In the dim light under the trees Bishop caught a glimpse of what looked like a deep overhang in the side of the mountain ahead of them. A flash of lightning showed him that was exactly what he'd seen. He reined Streak in that direction, fighting the wind that now had a few rain-drops in it.

The cut in the side of the mountain was almost a cave with a very wide opening. It was deep enough that the animals could be brought in for shelter as well as all of them. It was in the south side of the mountain. With the rain coming in from the north, it shouldn't blow far into the shelter.

"Let's get as much firewood inside as we can," Bishop told the others. "It looks like we'll be here for the rest of the day."

For the next several minutes, all of them hurried to bring in limbs and drag up deadfalls to stack in out of the rain. By the time the storm rolled over the top of the moun-tain and began drenching the area outside of their over-hang, they had a good enough pile of wood to last through the day.

Bishop, Angelina, and Cruz stood back from the front of the overhang and watched the storm thrash and drown the trees outside the shelter. Lightning and thunder were almost constant.

"Looks like it's goin' to last most of the day," Cruz said.

"We might as well get some sleep if we can," Bishop said. "We need to rest anyway. Nobody's goin' to be movin' around in this storm."

BEHIND THEM, Upton had found a tiny overhang that was just enough for him to stay relatively dry. His horses and most of his equipment got soaked, however. He'd been fortunate enough to bring his bedroll in with him. All in all, he passed a miserable day.

20

A few hours later, Bishop awoke to the sound of a steady rain falling outside the overhang. Far off, he could still hear grumbles of thunder as the storm marched on past Mount Withington. He lay there beside Angelina and listened to her snore slightly for a few more minutes. Sleeping in the daytime had never been as refreshing for him as sleeping at night, so he felt a little groggy. From experience, he knew the brain fog would clear after several minutes. In the meantime, he decided to read some more from Thompkins' diary.

Carefully, he rolled out from under his blankets. He didn't want to disturb Angelina if he could help it. Once on his feet, he glanced around at the other men still rolled in their blankets.

Greer lay on his back, snoring loudly. *I must've been a lot more tired than I thought to be able to sleep through that much noise,* Bishop realized.

Potts lay with his head completely covered by his blankets, maybe to dampen the sound of Greer's snoring. It seemed to have worked.

Cruz lay on his back, also, but his head and shoulders were elevated by lying back on his saddle. That apparently kept him from snoring.

A glance at the animals in the back of the overhang showed all of them standing three-legged, at least dozing.

Bishop stepped back over to his saddle bags, which he decided to keep close to him when he slept. The unknown intruder from the other night showed him the need to do this. He took out the diary and found a sandy place to sit and lean against the wall of the shelter. Carefully, he teased apart a few more pages and began to read.

It has been a couple of days since I wrote anything, and some things have happened. We rode across a wide plain one night to get to the mountain where we now are camped. It is called Madre Mountain and is supposed to be the one where the canyon filled with gold is located.

Sharpe says this is the mountain, but I don't know whether to believe him or not. According to him and that map that he lets no one else see, this is the third mountain where the canyon is supposed to be.

The other men continue to argue with Sharpe about seeing the map. I guess they still believe it actually shows the location of the canyon. Sharpe continues to camp slightly apart from the rest of us, but not quite as far away as at first. I believe he may not have as much confidence in the map as at first, either.

I have seen Sharpe talking to Alito more and more, seeming to rely on him for directions. Does this mean he has no idea where we're going? If so, I don't think depending on a half-Apache to guide us is a good idea. It would make a lot more sense to agree this expedition is a failed one and return home while we're all still in one piece.

At least, we have not run into any more Apaches. There have been signs of them around, but nothing really fresh. At least according to Alito.

Alito has been spending more time taking off on his own recently. When I asked Charlie about this, he said Sharpe told him the man was looking for the best way to get to the canyon. But I don't know if this is really what he's doing. No one has said for sure the canyon is on this mountain. Or if it is, exactly where. If Alito knows where it is, why hasn't he told Sharpe? And if he perhaps has told Sharpe, why hasn't he told the rest of us?

This makes me wonder a couple of things. First, is Alito meeting with the Apaches to set up an ambush for all of us? Possibly, he is doing exactly what Sharpe said. But there has always been something about the man that rubs me the wrong way. Is that my prejudice against him because he's half-Apache?

The second thing I wonder about is whether or not Sharpe has a plan to get the gold for himself and not share it at all. His actions concerning the map seem to point that way. Or maybe he had that idea in the beginning when his confidence in the map was higher, but now that it seems to have decreased, maybe he has entered into an agreement with Alito. An agreement that might have to do with Alito leading us into an ambush that only he and Sharpe survive. Then they could split the gold and ride away.

I think these things when trying to go to sleep, and they seem so potentially possible. Then, in the daylight, I consider them again, and they sound like the makings of a cheap dime novel. I don't know what is happening, but I do know this: If I had all this to do over again, I would not have left Lottie. I would have found something, anything, to do that was honest work. I believe we could have made it somehow.

Now, I just hope to get home to her again.

Bishop leaned back against the rock wall of the over-hang and closed his eyes, listening to the rain outside. He felt like he'd been reading the words of a man who had some kind of sense that he wouldn't make it out of this wilderness alive. The same wilderness in which he was sitting.

Is that what happened to Thompkins? he asked himself. *Did he really have some kind of warning about what was comin' for him? I know that can happen. Back in the war I heard men say they felt like they wouldn't make it out of the battle we were going to be in the next day, and they didn't. It was like they knew they were goin' to die. So I believe Thompkins might have had that same kind of feeling.*

He saw Potts stirring, then pushing aside his blankets. For a few seconds, the man moved his head around the interior of he overhang as if reminding himself of where he was. Then he stood, went to the corner of the overhang away from everyone else and relieved himself. When he came back to the sleeping area, he spotted Bishop.

Bishop motioned him over to sit beside him. When Potts hunkered down close to him, Bishop asked, "When you were here before, what did you think about that half-Apache, Alito?"

Potts picked up a small stick from the floor of the shelter and began scratching in the dirt with it. "I never did trust that man. Never did figger out why Sharpe wanted him with us, either. At least not at first. Toward the last, I began thinkin' maybe Sharpe didn't trust that map he had, so he leaned more on Alito to tell him where we needed to go."

Bishop considered this, then asked, "Did you ever think Alito was meetin' with the Apaches and settin' you up for an ambush? Thompkins mentioned him ridin' out from your camp from time to time."

"Yeah, that was strange. I mean, we were in Apache country, and the guide rides off. That can't be good. But Sharpe said he was lookin' for the best way to get to that gold canyon. I guess all of us were so ready to find that gold that we'd believe just about anything. But then I thought if he knew where the canyon was, why didn't he just take us

there, and let all of us find the best way into it? I believe
that half-breed set us up with those Apaches on this here
mountain."

"Sure sounds like he could've done that," Bishop
agreed. "Have you remembered anything else since we've
got here?"

"I'm beginnin' to remember some landmarks. Don't
remember this overhang, though. We must've come in a
different way. But I don't remember just where I got separated from Ernest yet."

While they were talking, Bishop noticed Cruz get up
and walk outside the shelter. The rain had stopped, but
clouds still covered the sky.

Cruz came back in at the end of Bishop's conversation
with Potts. "Bishop, come take a look."

Bishop got to his feet, his knees popping, and followed
Cruz. They went to a place where they could remain
hidden, but could look out over the bare plain.

"Out there about a half mile or so," Cruz said, pointing
almost straight out from them. "Somethin's movin'."

Bishop followed the direction Cruz pointed and
watched. In another minute, he caught the movement Cruz
was talking about. It was too far to tell for sure what was
moving, but there few choices. It could be animals of some
kind, but few animals he knew of other than pronghorn
antelope would be moving around out in the open like that.
More likely it was Apaches.

And from what he could tell, they seemed to be headed right for them.

"Go wake ever'body," Bishop told Cruz. "I'll stay here and watch that movement for a while. Maybe I can tell who it is."

A few minutes later, he was sure who was moving around out on the plain.

Back in the shelter, he explained the situation to the rest. "There are Apaches ridin' this way. They don't seem to be in a hurry, so I don't think they were follerin' our tracks. But they were comin' right toward us. Hopefully, they'll go on to another part of the mountain, but we've got to be ready if they don't. Let's move all the packs and saddles up here to make a sort of fort in case they find us and decide to attack."

Greer spoke up. "Why don't we saddle up and ride off? Seems to me that would be better than waitin' here to see if they find us."

Bishop explained. "If we stay here, we won't make any tracks for them to find. I think that storm wiped out any tracks we left gettin' here. Plus, ridin' out would be movement that the Apaches could see, just like Cruz saw their movement." He shook his head. "I think stayin' here beats tryin' to get away."

The half-breed looked like he wanted to say more, but didn't. He just hung his head and walked to the place where he left his saddle.

A few minutes later, they had done all they could to get ready for the Apaches, if the Indians did find them. They lay down behind their hasty breastwork and waited. Bishop worried about the horses and Streak. If the Apaches found them, all of the animals were in danger of being wounded or killed by bullets ricocheting off the rock walls of the overhang. But there was nothing he could do about that.

While they waited, the clouds flew on overhead, driven by winds up high that pushed them hard. The sun came out only a little bit before it disappeared behind the mountains to the west of them. When it set, it lit up the sky with an amazing red color that reflected off the tail-ends of the clouds that were left.

Darkness was nearly complete before Bishop said, "I don't think they're goin' to find us. Angelina, why don't you make us some supper? Be sure to keep the fire low. No more than you absolutely need." While she went farther into the shelter to take care of supper, he told the others, "We'll have to be alert tonight. We'll have two of us stand guard at a time, one at each end of the opening to the shelter. Let's say three hours at a time. That means we won't get a lot of sleep, but that's better than bein' dead."

21

The night passed without any sign of Apaches. While that wasn't a guarantee there were none around, it did make Bishop feel better about those they saw the day before. Apparently, the ones they saw riding toward them went to a different part of the mountain. They still would need to be careful and very watchful.

As they were getting ready to get underway exploring the mountain, Potts came up to Bishop. "I've remembered where I got separated from Ernest. We got into another fight with the Apaches. It's not far from here."

"Okay. Lead the way." As he said this, Bishop promised himself he'd keep an eye on Potts. He still wasn't sure about the man or about how much he'd said was the truth.

They started off, headed north around Madre Mountain. Potts led them along a narrow game trail.

"I remember this trail," he said after they rode about a mile. "We came up on the mountain just a little piece back and found it. That's why the overhang wasn't familiar to me. We came in this way and follered the trail."

After an hour of riding, Potts brought them to a halt at the edge of a little clearing. The clearing was about an acre in size ending at a bare mountain slope that was too steep to climb.

"This is where we had that fight with the Apaches," Potts said, pointing over toward the steep mountainside.

"Is this where you got separated from Thompkins?" Bishop asked.

"No, but it's where that all got started. Alito told us the Apaches were comin', so we forted up over against the mountain." Potts started across the open area toward the mountainside. As they got closer, he said, "You can see where we pulled those trees over to give us cover. There were six of us then." He paused for a few seconds, then went on. "The Apaches came at us from here. I'd say there was a dozen of 'em. We killed two or three when they came chargin' out of the trees toward us. But the rest of 'em got into the grass, and we couldn't see 'em. They started shootin', and we couldn't see what to shoot back at. This is where Nolan Sharpe and Dixon Howard were killed. Both of 'em shot through the head. None of us could tell where the shots came from, either. I thought for sure this was where I'd breathe my last."

"How did you get away from here?" Cruz asked.

"We held out 'til dark, then Alito came to me and Ernest. He had Arthur Ripley with him. He showed us a little trail and told us to foller him. Somehow, that trail led past the Apaches. We got prob'ly three hundred yards or a little more away from this clearing and settled down for the rest of the night. Near as I could tell we were in a little hollow. I've never been so scared in my life, I don't mind tellin' you. And dark? I literally couldn't see my hand in front of my face. Alito told us to stay still and quiet. So that's what we did. I guess we were all just plain wore out from fightin' those Apaches and bein' so scared. All of us went to sleep. All of us other than Alito. I don't think he ever slept. I woke up a couple of times in the night, and he was always awake. Once, he was comin' back into the hollow from somewhere. Prob'ly out scoutin' those Apaches, I guess."

When Potts paused like he was thinking back on what he went through, Bishop said, "So it was just you, Thompkins, Ripley, and Alito left?"

Potts jerked like he'd been startled, then nodded. "Yeah, just the four of us. But when daylight came, Ripley was gone."

"Gone? Where'd he go in the middle of the night?" That

didn't sound right to Bishop, but he wanted to hear Potts' explanation.

"We asked Alito that. He said Ripley left in the middle of the night. Just got up from where he was layin' and walked out. When we asked Alito why he didn't stop him, the man just shrugged and said he thought maybe Ripley was needin' to use the bushes. Said when Ripley didn't come back, he wasn't goin' to take the risk of goin' after him."

"You ever think this Alito did somethin' to Ripley?"

Potts looked out over the clearing, then focused on Bishop again. "Yeah, I thought about that, but not 'til after I was back home. And then I wondered why he didn't do somethin' to the rest of us, too, if he did somethin' to Ripley."

Bishop nodded. "That's a good question. There's a lot you can't understand about Indians of any kind. So when did you get separated from Thompkins?"

Potts picked up his story again. "When it was good and light, Alito started leadin' us off the mountain. Me and Ernest were pretty much done with tryin' to find the gold that was supposed to be on this mountain. All we wanted right then was to get back home. About a hundred yards along, we found Ripley. He was layin' on his back in the middle of this little trail we follered. All his clothes had been cut off of him and tossed over to one side. His arms and legs were tied to trees alongside the trail and a leg of his long johns was stuffed in his mouth. The Apaches had gouged out his eyes and cut off his nose. There was blood ever'where. It looked like they'd cut him all over his chest and belly." Potts paused, looked out across the clearing again, swallowed hard, then went on. "They, they cut off his private parts, too." He turned back to Bishop. "I think he was alive when they did that. There was a lot of blood between his legs. And his throat had been cut almost from ear to ear."

They all went quiet when Potts finished his story of finding Ripley. None of them wanted to think about what Ripley went through at the hands of the Apaches, but none of them could get the image of what his body would've looked like out of their heads.

"What did you do then?" Bishop asked.

Potts sighed. "We wanted to bury Ripley, but Alito said there wasn't time. The Apaches could come back at any time. The noise of trying to dig a grave when we had nothing to dig with would've brought the Apaches right to us. So we went on. We stopped once to rest, and Alito went back along the trail to see what he could see. He came back only a few minutes later and told us the Apaches were comin'. We ran. Finally, Alito said we had to stop and fight again. That's where I got separated from Ernest. It's not too far from here."

"Okay, take us there," Bishop said.

They rode down the trail Potts said they took from the

clearing. Like he told them, about three hundred yards later he showed them the hollow where Ripley disappeared. Another hundred yards along the trail, he stopped.

"This is where we found Ripley." He pointed to a spot on the trail. Off to one side lay the remnants of Ripley's clothing. There was no sign of the body left.

"Animals took care of the body," Cruz said. "We could prob'ly find some bones here and there if we looked for them."

"No need to," Bishop said. "What would we do with 'em other than put 'em in a hole, if we found any? That sounds cold, I know. But it's the way it has to be."

"The spot where we had the last fight with the Apaches and where I got separated from Ernest ain't far ahead." Potts started off again, the rest of them following.

Another quarter mile farther, Potts stopped again at the edge of an old rockslide. The slide was about fifty yards wide and covered the side of the mountain from far above them to a long way below where they stood.

"It was here," Potts said. "Alito told us the Apaches were comin', so we got into those rocks over at the far edge of this slide. We knew they'd come right along here, so we hoped to fight 'em off and maybe make 'em leave us alone." He gazed off toward the rocks. "It didn't turn out that way. We held 'em off for a while, but some of 'em got above us. Ernest worked his way up a little bit to see if he could drive 'em off from up there. I don't know where Alito was. I lost sight of him just before the shootin' started. Those Apaches just didn't want to give up and go away. They started gettin' real close to us, so I called out to Ernest to get back on the trail and run. I turned to do the same thing and saw he'd dropped that diary. I knew he'd want it back, so I picked it up, stuck it inside my shirt, and took off runnin'. That's when I got shot." He pointed to the bandage over his ear. "Knocked me on my butt, but I wasn't goin' to let them Apaches get me, so I jumped up and ran. Never saw Alito or Ernest again. To this day, I don't know how I got away from those Apaches. I just remember runnin' then sort of wakin' up at home."

"You still don't remember how you got back home?" Bishop asked, trying not to sound like he thought Potts was lying.

"No idea," Potts responded, shaking his head. "But I must've had help or somehow caught a horse. I rode a horse into town when I came back. People have told me that."

"That's quite a story, Potts," Bishop said, just a hint of doubt slipping in.

Potts heard the doubt. "You don't have to believe it, Bishop. But it's the truth. That's what happened."

"All right. Let's take a break for somethin' to eat. Then we'll figger out what to do next."

. . .

UPTON CROUCHED under a cedar tree a mile behind and to the west of Bishop and the others. He watched as a band of six Apaches rode through a tiny clearing along the mountain trail they followed.

The day before, Upton had barely avoided running into probably this same band of Apaches when they rode into the trees where he was camped. They had to have come across that broad plain he crossed late the night before.

That close call scared him.

22

Bishop sent Greer back down their trail a little way to keep watch there for Apaches. Cruz began walking around, looking over the ground and trying to figure out what might've happened to Thompkins. As he searched, he chewed on a piece of jerky.

Bishop liked to watch Cruz work. He would walk slowly around an area, stopping every once in a while to look at something or to pick something up. While he watched his partner, Cruz stopped, knelt down and looked closely at something, then stood and looked off in the direction they had been going. He walked a little farther that way, knelt down again, then stood and came over to Bishop.

"Looks like somebody was up in those rocks. Signs of somebody wearin' boots, but lots of signs of moccasins, too.

Some of the tracks are pretty fresh. Most of them are old, maybe as much as a month. There hasn't been much rain, so the impressions are still here and there. I'd say somebody walked out that way." He pointed in the direction they had been going. "I don't know if the tracks belonged to Thompkins, but I know the fresher ones didn't. They were a flat boot like miners usually wear."

Bishop looked off down the trail where Cruz pointed, then turned back to him. "You think there's somebody else out here lookin' for that canyon with the gold in it?"

"Could be. If that's what it is, he's leavin' a lot of tracks. That might be good for us or bad for us. Good, if he goes a different way than we're goin', and the Apaches foller him. Bad, if he goes the way we're goin', and the Apaches foller him. They'd be more likely to find us, too." Cruz turned toward the trail for a second, then back to Bishop. "And it sure looks like that miner's goin' right where we were headed."

Before either of them could say more, Greer came back to them. He was almost running.

"Apaches!" he gasped, out of breath. "I went a little over a quarter mile back." He had to stop and catch his breath. "Back where I could see a little way back down the trail. They're comin'! About a half mile back behind us now."

"How many of 'em?" Bishop asked as Cruz started helping to get everything together.

"I ain't sure. I just saw maybe six. They didn't look like they were follerin' a trail, so maybe they won't find our tracks."

"They won't find tracks if we don't leave any." Bishop got Cruz' attention. "We need a place to hide. Ride on down the trail and see if you can find somethin'. And hurry. We ain't got much time."

When everyone had everything packed up, Bishop sent them on down the trail. He stayed behind and tried to over up as much of the sign that they'd been there as he could. After he finished, he looked the area over. He'd done the best he could given the short amount of time he had to get it done. He'd scattered sand over their tracks, being careful to let it sift out between his fingers. It wouldn't fool the Apaches for very long if they were looking for tracks, but maybe it would at least slow them down.

He reined Streak around and started after the others. About two hundred yards farther on, he spotted Cruz sitting his horse in the middle of the small trail.

"I found a bench up on the side of the mountain," he explained when Bishop came up to him. He jerked a thumb over his shoulder. "Just around the bend ahead there's a real small game trail that leads up to it. I sent the rest on up there."

"Okay," Bishop said. "Lead the way."

They rode quickly to the bend. Like Cruz said, just

beyond it was a tiny trail that led off to the left. The under-brush there was thin, so they pushed through it with no problem. Once they were through, Cruz dismounted and wove the limbs of the small bushes and saplings together so the gap where the small trail left the slightly larger one wouldn't be so obvious. He reached out under the bushes and sifted dirt over the end of the trail. Hopefully, that would keep the Apaches from seeing that there was even a trail there. Then he mounted up and led Bishop to the bench he found. The little trail climbed higher on the side of the mountain.

The bench on the side of the mountain was about forty yards long and ten yards wide. A screen of bushes grew up right on the edge of the bench, making it difficult to see from below. When Bishop went to the edge and looked over, he saw the trail almost a hundred feet below him.

"With any luck, the Apaches won't see us or even see the bench up here," he said to Cruz. "How did you find it?"

"When I saw where the trail up here led off the other trail, I thought maybe there was a cave or some rocks or somethin' up this way, so I follered it up here. Only thing wrong with this place is that there's no way out except the way we came in."

Bishop nodded, then walked back to the others. "We might have a chance to avoid those Apaches if we can keep quiet up here. Chances are good that they'll ride on by down below us. But if they find us, we'll have to fight.

There's no trail out of here other than the one we came in on." He watched as the realization of the seriousness of their situation took hold. "Angelina, you stay with the animals. Try to keep 'em quiet. Greer and Potts, you come with me. We'll spread out along the bench and keep those Apaches from gettin' up here. Now, I want you to hear this loud and clear: Don't either one of you shoot unless I do. We're goin' to let them Apaches go on by if they will. We ain't goin' to start a shootin' war with 'em." He met the eyes of both of the men, trying to determine if both of them heard what he said. It looked to him like they did. "Okay, you two go over to Cruz. He'll put you in position."

When the two men were gone, Bishop walked over to Angelina and took her in his arms. For a long minute, he just held her.

"Is it going to be bad?" she asked, her head buried in his chest.

"It could be, if the Apaches find us. But I think we've got a good chance to stay hid and avoid trouble." He pushed her back enough to meet her eye. "In case they find us, and we can't drive 'em off, use your pistol. Don't let yourself get caught by those Indians."

After a long kiss, he stepped away from her and went to his place on the edge of the bench.

Lying on his belly, Bishop could see the trail below from under the bushes that concealed him. For several very long minutes, he heard nothing, saw nothing. In the distance, the wind blew through the pines on the side of the mountain making that moaning sound that had provided him with a soothing noise to lull him to sleep on many nights. Far off, the 'skree' of a hunting hawk gliding across the thermals came to his ears. An ant crawled across the back of his hand.

A minute later, Cruz got his attention with a tiny grunt. Slowly, Bishop turned his head toward his partner, knowing sudden movements caught the eye in situations such as those. Cruz nodded slowly in the direction of the trail to their right.

Bishop's eyes caught a movement on the trail. Seconds later, a mounted Apache rode into view around the bend in the trail. From what Bishop could see, he was a short man with sun-darkened skin, black hair with a tan headband, and wearing a light-colored shirt. His legs were naked other than high moccasins that were tied to his calves. He carried a rifle with the butt resting on his thigh, the barrel pointed skyward. He gave the impression of being alert to the point of nothing getting past him. This last was just a thought Bishop had, possibly due to being in such a precarious situation.

Behind him came another, then another, and another. Six of them in all. Every one a warrior. Every one dangerous.

Bishop found himself holding his breath, waiting for one of them to either glance down and see the tiny trail leading up to their bench or to look up and see his face. Consciously, he willed the Apaches to ride on by, not to look up or to glance down.

For a very long five minutes, the Indians rode slowly past them. Clearly, they were not looking for Bishop and the others. They were just riding through their domain.

When the last Apache rode past, Bishop let out a long, slow breath. He motioned to Greer and Potts to stay quiet and not move. He wanted to be sure the Apaches were out of hearing range of them.

Several minutes later, he scooted back from the edge and got to his feet. "I think they're far enough away so they can't hear us," he said. "But we still need to keep the noise down as much as we can."

They gathered back at the animals with Angelina.

"Do you think they'll come back this way?" Greer asked.

"Prob'ly not," Bishop said. "But I think we should spend the night here and make sure they're long gone before we venture out again. We'll take a look around the mountain tomorrow."

They set about making camp. Angelina made a stew out of shaved jerky, wild onions, and some rice they had left.

Potts went looking along the wall of the bench while waiting on supper. At one place, he pulled out his knife and dug out a few nuggets of gold. They were small, but they were gold. He carried them back to the others.

"I found gold!" Excitement colored his words. "Maybe there's somethin' to that story about a canyon full of gold on this mountain!"

"Or more likely that's all the gold on this mountain," Bishop said.

"You're just sayin' that because you want to find that canyon yourself and keep all the gold!" Potts' eyes grew wide as he gazed at the small gold nuggets again. "I say let's stay right here for a few days and see how much gold we can find. It's a good place to stay hid from those Apaches."

Greer joined in. "Potts is right! This here might be the mother lode for all we know! We can dig right here, find all the gold we can carry, then ride out of here without those Apaches knowin' anything about it!"

Bishop began to get concerned because both Potts and Greer were beginning to get louder in their enthusiasm. "You two need to listen and listen real close. Even right now you're gettin' loud enough for any Apaches close by to hear and come down on us. What then? Besides that, you don't have any tools to dig with. And if you did, the diggin' would make too much noise."

"We don't need tools," Potts countered. "I dug these out with my knife. Why, I'll bet we could use knives and dig out enough gold to live for a year!"

"You don't know any such thing!" Bishop made his voice harder. "All you know is you found a few little gold nuggets. Did you see any more wherever you dug these out? You just got lucky, that's all."

Potts' eyes narrowed. "Maybe so, but you're jealous. Jealous I found this gold. And you want to make us go on from here, then come back and claim all the gold here for yourself! You'll prob'ly make us go on with you and figger out a way to kill us so me'n Greer can't come back." He stepped back, his hand hovering over his pistol. "I'll tell you right now, I ain't goin' to give up this spot. It's mine! Mine and Greer's, since he's my partner. I'm stakin' claim to it right now. All of you are witnesses! This here's my claim!"

Bishop held up both hands, palms out toward Potts. "Okay, okay. Listen, you can have this spot. As far as I'm concerned, you can have this whole mountain. I don't want any of the gold. But if you draw and shoot that gun, it'll bring ever' Apache within two miles down on us. Then nobody will get any gold. Now is that the way you want it?"

Watching the emotions play over Potts' face would've been funny if it weren't for the circumstances. Clearly, thinking wasn't his strong suit, but just as clearly he tried and tried hard to wrap his mind around all that Bishop said. Finally, after a couple of minutes, he relaxed.

"All right. We'll keep on helpin' you look for Ernest." Potts said this in a calm voice. Then a great frown creased his forehead and pulled his eyebrows together over his nose. "But when that's done, me'n Greer are comin' back here and gettin' all the gold we can find. Then we'll pick up all the gold we can carry in that canyon that I know is around here somewhere."

"All right. Now, we need to eat. Then we'll wait out the rest of the day to make sure those Apaches ain't around anywhere close."

23

With no return of the Apaches through the rest of that day, Bishop and the others spent a quiet night. Just to be safe, they kept a guard at the edge of the bench through the night.

Bishop took the last guard shift of the night, figuring that if the Apaches knew where they were, that would be the time they would attack. He watched the day begin in the east with the sky growing gradually lighter over the mountains. When nothing happened as daylight replaced darkness, he began to relax more. By the time he could see the rays of the sun reaching over the horizon, setting the stage for the sun's return, he knew they were safe. For the time being.

Behind him, he heard the others stirring. Before long, the pleasing smells of coffee and bacon wafted over him.

His mouth watered at the expectation of digging into the bacon and holding the hot cup full of black coffee in his hands.

He stood from where he'd been sitting and walked to the fire. Angelina greeted him with a smile that lit up her eyes.

"That sure smells good," he told her after a kiss.

"I hope it tastes as good as it smells." She poured him a cup of coffee. "It'll be ready in just a few minutes."

He stepped over to Cruz. "I think we should split up again today. We can cover more ground faster. I don't know about you, but I'm really ready to get out of here."

"You think it's a smart idea to split up?"

Bishop sipped his coffee. "Yeah, I think it'll be okay. Those Apaches are somewhere else by now. They might even have gone back to one of those other mountains. Anyway, by splitting up, we won't raise as much dust and will prob'ly be less likely to be seen."

Cruz thought for a moment. "Okay. Makes sense. After breakfast?"

"Yeah. I'll tell the others."

As he should have expected, Potts and Greer, mostly Potts, didn't like the idea of splitting up.

"You're just tryin' to get rid of us so you can come back and get whatever gold is here," Potts said. Greer stood behind him, shaking his head and glaring at Bishop. "You want to split up so those Apaches will catch me'n Greer and kill us. Then you'll get the gold."

Bishop thought for a moment, then said, "Okay. Then you and Greer stay here while we go search the mountain. We'll be sure to come back and tell you when we find that canyon filled with gold."

It was fascinating to Angelina to watch how Potts' face changed as he thought about that. At first, he wasn't quite sure what Bishop was saying. Then, as he thought about it more, he grasped the idea that they could find the gold canyon, take the gold, and leave. His face was all squinted up while he thought about this. Thinking was hard work for him. Then, his face brightened, his eyebrows rose from where they'd been almost touching over his nose, and a grin began and died under the scraggly mustache he'd grown.

"Oh, no! No, no! We're not goin' to let you get all that gold for yourself. We'll go off around the mountain the other way. And I'm goin' to tell you this." He pointed his finger right at Bishop's nose. "When we, me'n Greer, find that canyon full of gold, we ain't goin' to come back and let you know. No sir! We're goin' to load up all we can carry and get out of here. From here on, it's ever' man for hisself. Now how do you like that?"

Bishop hung his head for a second, then lifted it and met Potts' eye again. "Well, if that's the way you want it, Potts, I guess that's the way it'll be."

"Damn right that's the way I want it!"

When breakfast was over, they cleaned up and got ready to move out. "We'll search the mountain until the middle of the day, then meet back here," Bishop said. "Me, Angelina, and Cruz will go on around north. Greer and Potts, you two go south."

Potts and Greer took off quickly. When they were out of sight, Cruz said, "I don't trust that Potts. There's somethin' awful sneaky about him."

"Yeah, there is," Bishop agreed. "I don't trust him, either. Never have. I can't put my finger on it, but I know he ain't bein' truthful about somethin'."

They started out and rode for a little over an hour when they came to a wide valley. A mile or more later Bishop pulled them to a stop. "It looks like a canyon up ahead. Let's go take a look."

They rode into a deep cut in the side of the mountain. The bottom of the canyon was filled with cedar and pine trees. A trail led right down the middle of the canyon, winding around boulders that looked like they had rolled down the steep sides at some time in the past. The canyon was a good hundred yards wide for most of its length.

Cruz got Bishop's attention at one point and pulled to a stop. He pointed down at something on the ground. "Tracks. Looks like somebody wearin' boots." He dismounted and knelt down to study the tracks more closely. "They look a lot like those tracks I found back where that rockslide was. Like miner's boots."

"When do you figger they were made?"

"Not that long ago. Maybe a day, maybe less." Cruz stood and looked ahead of them in the canyon. "They're headed on into the canyon."

Cruz climbed aboard his horse again, and the trio rode on farther. Twenty yards on into the canyon, Bishop stopped again. This time, he pointed over toward one wall of the canyon.

"Does that look like somebody's been diggin' over there?"

"It sure does," Cruz said.

They continued on into the canyon. At that point, they hadn't seen any gold nuggets laying on the ground just waiting to be picked up, but Bishop hadn't thought they would find any. Still, it had been nice to dream about such a thing.

Bishop heard the sound of falling water ahead of them. When he turned, he saw that both Cruz and Angelina had heard it, too. The sound grew louder as they continued on. A few more yards, and the canyon opened up. A short waterfall flowed out of the end of the canyon about thirty yards in front of them. The water made a small pool with a stream flowing out of it. The stream disappeared into a split in the side of the canyon.

What was even more surprising was the cabin built of

rock that sat at the end of the canyon close to the water. They stopped several yards in front of the cabin. Bishop called out, "Hello, the cabin! Anybody there?"

No one answered. With a glance at Cruz and Angelina, Bishop nudged Streak in the ribs and rode up to the front of the cabin. Boot prints were plentiful in the dirt before the door. He dismounted and pounded on the door so his knocking would be heard above the sounds of the waterfall. No one answered.

Bishop pushed on the door. It wasn't locked and swung open on leather strap hinges. Inside, the cabin showed plenty of signs of being lived in. A fire smoldered in a rock fireplace, a cot sitting against the back wall held blankets, and the smell of old coffee hit his nose. He walked back outside.

"Somebody lives here," he said.

"They sure do," came a voice from the corner of the cabin away from them. "I live here. I'm comin' out now. Be sure you don't shoot me."

A man a little past middle age stepped around the corner. He held a shotgun pointed at the ground at Bishop's feet. Even if he got shot, the man could lift the double barrels and get off a shot. At that range, Bishop would be cut in half.

The man glanced from one to the other of them. "I'm Marlon Hightower. Been minin' this mountain for five years now."

"I'm John Bishop, this is my wife, Angelina, and my partner, Cruz Andrus. If you don't mind me askin', how have you kept from gettin' killed, Mr. Hightower?"

Hightower grinned, showing a couple of missing teeth. "Right from the first when I come onto this mountain, I knowed I'd have to deal with the Apaches one way or another. And I knowed fightin' 'em wasn't the way. There was way too many of them and only one of me. So I hunted 'em down and talked to their head man. Told him I was only interested in gold, the yellow rock. Nothin' else. Told him I'd stay here for six summers, then go away and never come back. Somehow, that made sense to him. Maybe he was in a good mood or somethin', I don't know. But he agreed. Six summers, that's all. This summer's number six, so I gotta leave if I don't want to be planted here."

Bishop nodded. "I reckon you've heard about the canyon that's supposed to be somewhere on this mountain. One that's covered in gold nuggets just layin' there, waitin' to be picked up."

Hightower laughed, a high, cackling laugh. "There ain't no such canyon on this mountain or any other one around here. I ought'a know. I've been on all of 'em."

"You certainly have found a beautiful canyon here, Mr. Hightower," Angelina said.

"Yep. And I've found a little gold, too. But ain't none of it been layin' on the ground. It's all been down deep in the ground. I've had to dig out ever' last nugget with lots of back breakin' work." He paused, just long enough to look at the three of them. "Why are you folks out here? You sure ain't here to look for gold. You got no tools to dig with, and you don't seem like the kind who'd believe some fool notion about nuggets just layin' on the ground."

"We're lookin' for a man who came out here about six weeks ago," Bishop said. "He was with some other men who were lookin' for that canyon with the gold nuggets. His wife asked us to come find him or find his body, what might be left of it. His name was Ernest Thompkins."

Hightower thought for a moment. "About six weeks ago, you say?" When Bishop nodded, he went on. "Yeah, I remember seein' them once. Then when I saw 'em again, there was only two of 'em. Just saw 'em at a distance. I did find a body at the mouth of the canyon out there. I reckon it was one of them. Like I said, I only saw 'em at a distance. I buried him back where I found him. He was shot in the back at close range. Want me to show you?"

"Yeah, we'd like that."

"Let me fetch somethin' in the cabin you prob'ly want, too." Hightower darted inside the cabin, then returned a minute later with a leather wallet. "That feller had this on him when I found him. I figgered I might try to find his kin after I leave this summer and give it to them. But I reckon you can do that, since his wife hired you to find him."

Bishop took the stained wallet and opened it up. Inside, the initials E.T. were burned into the leather. "E.T., Ernest

Thompkins. I think we know what happened now." Bishop found a couple of folded pages that looked like they were torn from the diary he had. The paper looked exactly the same. He unfolded them and read out loud.

This is the last will and testament of Ernest Thompkins. I swear I am of sound mind, but very damaged body. What I'm writing is true. Charlie Potts, my cousin, shot me and left me for dead. By the time somebody finds this, I will be dead. I pray whoever finds it will bury me proper and try to let my wife, Lottie, know. She lives in Albuquerque. I leave everything I have, which is little enough, to her. Charlie thought I had found gold and was keeping it secret from him. When I wouldn't tell him where it is, he shot me in the back. I swear we never found any gold.

Everyone was quiet when Bishop finished. It was almost as if now that they knew what happened to Thompkins there was a let-down. With Bishop, there also was that sense of betrayal to find out Potts had killed his own cousin over gold that neither of them had.

"I know you always had the feelin' that Potts wasn't bein' truthful with you," Cruz told Bishop. "Now we know why he wasn't."

"Yeah. I reckon we're goin' to have to have a talk with Potts." Bishop re-folded the papers, stuck them back in the wallet, and handed it to Angelina. "Why don't you hang onto this?" Then he turned to Hightower. "Do you mind showin' us where you buried Thompkins now?"

"Sure thing. Just foller me."

Hightower led them back the way they came into the canyon, but branched off before he got all the way to the mouth. A tiny trail led to a spot where two cedar trees grew and shaded a small cleared area. In the middle of that cleared area, a grave lay. Stones had been laid over it so the animals wouldn't get into it.

"There he is," Hightower said. "It was the best I could do. Stays shady all day and is protected from the worst of the weather."

"It's a real nice place, Mr. Hightower," Angelina said. "Thank you for taking care of Mr. Thompkins' body. We'll be sure to tell his wife he has a good place to be buried."

"I'm glad I could do that much. Now I've got to get back to work. I've only got a few months to go before I have to leave."

"We need to get goin', too," Bishop said. "Thanks again, Mr. Hightower."

24

After Hightower left, Bishop, Angelina, and Cruz stayed at the graveside for a while. It felt like the right thing to do, pay some respects to the man who only wanted for things to be better for his wife.

"It is sad that it turned out this way," Angelina said after a few minutes. "Mr. Thompkins was just trying to help himself and his wife. Then to be murdered like he was." She shook her head and wiped away a tear.

"It's goin' to be hard on Mrs. Thompkins, but at least she'll know what happened." Bishop sighed from the bottom of his lungs. "I guess now we can go back and let her know."

"Don't you want to make things right with Potts?" Cruz asked.

Bishop turned and gazed out across the opening to the

canyon for several moments. Then he focused on Cruz and Angelina. "No. It's not worth it. If Mrs. Thompkins wants to do somethin' about him after she finds out what he did, then that's somethin' for the law to tend to. I think we just need to go home."

They mounted up and headed out of the canyon. At the mouth of the canyon, Cruz called out, "You two go on. I'll catch up. I think my horse got a rock in his hoof."

Bishop waved his understanding, and he and Angelina kept going. They got about fifty yards farther when the shooting started.

With the echoing of the sounds of the shots, Bishop couldn't place where they came from at first. He could tell there were at least two rifles shooting at them. One of the first bullets clipped his hat brim. Another one burned through his left leg from the top of the thigh and feeling like it went clear through.

When he grunted and grasped his leg, Angelina saw the blood and cried out, "John!"

"Ride!" he yelled. "Ride fast and don't slow down! We've got to get out of range!"

With his left hand clamped down on the wound he could see, Bishop pounded Streak's ribs with his right foot. Not used to being treated that way, Streak did exactly what Bishop wanted. He took off.

Bishop leaned over Streak's neck to cut down on wind resistance. A glance back at Angelina showed she was doing the same thing with her horse. They were no more than a few feet behind him.

He had no idea where Cruz was. Or if he was still alive.

They galloped for five minutes, putting more than a mile between them and whoever shot at them. Fortunately, the canyon was at the end of a valley where the ground was relatively flat. At the end of that time, Bishop slowed Streak down.

When Angelina caught up with him, she said, "John, are you hurt bad? There's blood all over your leg."

Bishop was just beginning to feel the real pain of his wound now. Before, the adrenaline from being shot at and being shot kept the pain at bay.

"They got me in the leg," he told her. "I think it went all the way through. Are you all right?"

"Yes, yes, I'm fine. But you're bleeding. I've got to stop the bleeding."

Bishop glanced behind them, saw no dust from anyone chasing them. Looking around, he saw a grove of trees a little distance from them.

"Let's get under cover in those trees. Then you can work on me."

Once inside the trees, Angelina dismounted and hurried over to Bishop. She helped him get down off Streak and made him sit down beside a tree.

One of the things they made sure to carry with each of them was enough clean material for bandages. Angelina got this from his saddle bag and got ready to wrap his leg to stop the bleeding.

"Take off your pants," she told him once she had the bandages ready.

"Are you sure this is the time and place?" Bishop asked, grinning.

For a second, Angelina didn't know what he was talking about. Then it registered. "You are not hurt too badly if you are thinking about such things now. You know what I mean."

"Yeah, I know. I don't think I could do much anyway. This hole in my leg hurts too much."

Once Angelina could see the wound in his leg better, she said, "The bullet did go all the way through just under the skin. That's good. I won't have to try to get it out of you. But you've lost a lot of blood."

"Get me bandaged up real good. We can't stay here. Those shots and all the dust we raised gettin' away from whoever was shootin' are sure to let all the Apaches on the mountain that we're here. We've got to find a place to hole up for a while. Help me get back on Streak."

"Is that a good idea? Shouldn't we wait here and make sure you're not bleeding any more?"

"We're not safe here. We need a good place to hide. You've got the bandages good and tight. Help me get up and on that mule."

No matter that it sent bolts of white-hot pain through

Bishop's leg, he knew he had to get mounted and get going. Gritting his teeth, he struggled to his feet with Angelina's help and then dragged himself onto Streak's back from the right side. Fortunately, all the mule did when Bishop climbed aboard from that side was look back at him. Once Angelina got mounted, they set off toward the end of the short valley. Bishop was looking for a cave or something like it where they would be out of sight.

They rode slowly, giving Bishop a chance to search the sides of the valley for anything that looked like a cave. Finally, at the very end of the valley, he spotted a dark spot on the side of the mountain ahead of them. It looked very small from a distance, but Bishop was beginning to feel light-headed from the loss of blood, so he decided to get closer and see if what he saw would work.

Up close, the dark spot turned into the mouth of a cave large enough for them and their animals. A screen of saplings and cedars concealed much of the opening. Riding up to it, they passed through a small forest of pines, their fallen needles covering the ground several inches thick. The thick ground cover would help hide their tracks.

Inside, Angelina helped him down and got him settled on the sandy floor of the cave. Then she unsaddled her horse and Streak and pulled the supplies off the pack horse whose reins she'd somehow held onto.

Winded from the exertion, she dropped to the sand beside Bishop. "After I rest for a minute, I will look at your bandages again." She paused, then went on. "What about Cruz?"

"I don't know," Bishop said, shaking his head. "He was behind us a little way. Maybe he was far enough back that whoever was shootin' at us didn't see him."

"Who do you think was doing the shooting?"

"I don't know. I don't think it was Apaches because there were only two rifles firin' at us. And Apaches would've chased us to finish us off." He paused, thinking. "Wonder if it was Potts and Greer? They were mad enough at me back on that bench that they might've figgered to get rid of me. Whoever it was will have to wait to finish what they started. I ain't goin' far with this bum leg."

25

Cruz lay beneath a short cedar tree on top of the canyon wall where they found Thompkins' grave. His horse was tied several yards behind him. He searched the far canyon wall and the area around it, moving only his eyes.

Whoever did that shootin' must be over on that other canyon wall, he told himself. *It was hard to tell just where they might be with all those echoes bouncin' around me, but that's got to be where they are. I hope Bishop and Angelina are okay. There wasn't no way for me to get to 'em.*

Like Bishop, he knew the sounds of rifle fire would attract the Apaches like flies to dog droppings. So he couldn't stay where he was much longer.

I'll wait five more minutes, then I've got to find a place to hide out. Maybe later I can go find Bishop and Angelina.

Minutes later, he spotted movement on the opposite canyon wall. The movement was brief, and he only got a glimpse, but it looked like two men hurried out of the rocks and out of sight. Then, movement at the mouth of the canyon below him caught his eye.

Apaches!

They had heard the rifle fire and came to see what they could find.

Although the Apaches were sixty yards away from him and lower, Cruz didn't move. Any movement could be seen and would lead them right to him.

The six Apaches rode warily forward toward the mouth of the canyon. Some of them searched the canyon wall across from Cruz with their eyes. Others searched his side of the canyon wall with their eyes. He knew the Apaches were as familiar with their territory as deer were with the square mile where they spent most of their lives. That meant anything out of place or different would get their attention. Slowly, he lowered his head so that only his eyes and the top of his head showed above the edge of the small depression where he lay.

Then, he waited.

A cloud drifted across the sun, bringing a bit of relief from the heat of the sun reflected from the rocks around him. The Apaches stopped almost just below him, looking and listening. One of their horses stomped a foot to get rid of a fly. Cruz hoped his horse wouldn't smell the Indian ponies below and call out to them. Fortunately, what wind there was blew down the canyon and away from them. A drop of sweat began at his hairline just above his nose and rolled down his face right between his eyes.

A minute later, the Apache that seemed to be in the lead said something in a low, guttural voice, and they rode on down the canyon. As soon as they were out of sight, Cruz let out the breath he wasn't aware he'd been holding. Slowly, he slid backward until out of sight of the canyon, then got to his feet.

Those Apaches won't stay down in the canyon, he told himself. *They'll come back out and climb up to search the top of the canyon walls, too. I need to be gone from here when they do.*

Gathering the reins of his horse, he led it slowly away from the canyon. After about fifty yards, he climbed on board his horse and rode through the trees and rocks looking for someplace he could hole up until the Apaches settled down and left the area.

He tried to ride on as much rock as possible. Even there, he'd leave tracks, but the Apaches would have to search for them. At least, it would slow them down if they found his tracks back at the canyon.

A quarter mile farther on, he found a place where a small trail at the end of long rocky stretched seemed to lead up the side of the mountain. It appeared not to have been used by anyone or any animals in some time. On impulse, Cruz decided to see where it led.

He reined his horse onto the trail and rode for a few yards, then stopped. He dismounted and tied the horse to a sapling beside the trail. Walking carefully on rocks as much as he could, he made his way back to the place where the trail started.

Since he'd been riding on a long sheet of rock for a long distance, there were no obvious tracks leading up to the small trail. For sure there were scars on the rock from his horse's hooves, but there was little he could do about that. But maybe he could do something about the tracks he left in the dirt of the small trail.

First, he tried to weave together the small branches of bushes that grew on either side of the trail to mask the opening of the trail. Then he gathered pine needles from spots as far away from the trail as he could reach and sprinkled them over the beginning of the trail. He also scattered twigs over the pine needles. When he was finished, he examined the spot carefully. It wasn't perfect, but maybe it would disguise the beginning of the trail enough for the Apaches to ride on past.

Once he was done with as much as he could do, Cruz walked back along the trail looking for any place where his horse had broken limbs from the bushes they passed. There was little he could do about them, if he found any, other than rub dirt on the stubs to make them less noticeable.

When he got to his horse, he climbed back into the

saddle and nudged the horse on up the tiny trail. They followed it for another quarter mile until it went around a shoulder of the mountain. At the same place, a large boulder had rolled down the mountainside at some time in the past and come to rest in front of a deep horizontal cut in the side of the mountain. It made a good place to stop and wait out the Apaches. If there was such a safe place.

Cruz had no illusions about his situation. He was hiding from Apaches in their home territory. And not only the Apaches, but also whoever shot at Bishop and Angelina. Whoever they were, they didn't hesitate to open fire knowing that Apaches were in the area. So, either they were determined to kill Bishop and Angelina or they felt confident enough to avoid running into the Apaches. And if they were that determined, then they would most likely come after Cruz as well.

Not only was he running for his life and hiding, he also had little food. Water wouldn't be a problem. He could find water when he needed it. But all the food he had was some jerky in his saddle bags. That would be enough for a couple of days, maybe longer if he only ate only a little at a time. But eventually he would have to figure out how to get some food.

Being alone never bothered him. He's been alone a lot in his short life, so he learned how to manage that. But he needed to find out if Bishop and Angelina were all right.

They were out in the open when the shooting started. One or both of them could've been hit, maybe even killed.

Who was doing the shooting? Cruz saw what he thought were two men hurrying out of the rocks across the canyon from him before the Apaches came. The only other two men he knew about who were in the same area were Potts and Greer.

Would they be stupid enough to shoot at Bishop knowing the Apaches would hear? From what he remembered of the discussion back on the bench, it was real likely that Potts would try to kill Bishop regardless of the Apaches. And Greer would go along with whatever Potts wanted.

Or was Potts smarter than anybody knew? Did he fire those shots, not caring whether they hit anybody or not? Did he know the shots would bring the Apaches here and away from that bench where he found those few nuggets?

Maybe he was counting on that. Bring the Apaches here so they could find and kill Bishop while Potts and Greer went back to that bench and dug for gold.

That could explain what happened. With no other white men in the area, it seemed to fit. Maybe those Apaches would find Potts' and Greer's tracks, follow them, and kill them.

Then another thought came to him. What about that other feller, Upton? Could he have been the one to fire the shots? But as far as they knew, Upton didn't have anybody with him. And Cruz was certain he saw two men scrambling over the rocks across the canyon from him. So probably it wasn't Upton doing the shooting.

I figger I know where Potts and Greer are now, but I wonder where Upton is?

JUST THEN, Daniel Upton lay in a little depression between two large rocks on a shelf about thirty feet above the six Apaches who had been riding around below him for the last hour. His horses were tied on the back side of the ridge behind him. That ridge jutted out from Madre Mountain about a hundred yards from the opening of the canyon where Bishop and the others had just been.

Upton followed them to the canyon, but didn't want to take the chance on being caught in there when those he followed rode back out. So he'd found the shelf and settled in to wait for them.

He was convinced that was the canyon where all the gold was supposed to be. His plan was to wait for Bishop and the others to ride back out, then follow them to a good ambush site. He planned to capture Bishop and the woman, then use her to make Bishop tell him where to find the gold. The other man with them he'd probably have to kill.

Then whoever it was started shooting. It looked to Upton like Bishop got hit, but he stayed in the saddle on that mule of his and rode off with the woman. He didn't know what happened to the other man.

Upton had been trapped on the shelf ever since.

He'd seen what Apaches did to white men they captured, so he didn't move or make a sound. The Apaches talked among themselves below him, then rode out into the valley, making sure they scanned every inch. In another few minutes, one of them got the attention of the rest, pointed down at the ground, and started off in the direction Bishop and the woman went.

I can't let those heathen redskins find Bishop, Upton realized. *If they do, I'll never get that diary and never find that canyon full of gold. Bishop and the rest rode out of this canyon like they'd found nothing, so I don't think it's the right one. I've got to get hold of that diary and see what's written in it. I know Sharpe and those others found the canyon, got the gold, and hid it. They were cheatin' me. So the location of that canyon or the location where they hid the gold has to be in that diary. I've got to get my hands on it.*

That's when he decided on a risky course of action. Those Apaches were almost two hundred yards away from him, getting close to being out of range of his Winchester. And it sure looked like they were on Bishop's trail.

He slipped off the shelf where he'd been hidden, made his way up to the top of the ridge, and found a place to rest the barrel of his rifle. Upton had been a sharpshooter in the war, so firing at distant targets was nothing new to him.

Once he had the rifle steady on its rest, he squeezed the trigger with equal pressure throughout his hand. Like it should have, the firing of the rifle came as a surprise to him. A little over two hundred yards away, one of the Apaches threw his arms in the air and tumbled off his pony.

Immediately, Upton levered another round into the Winchester's chamber and fired, not caring if he hit any of the Indians. He did the same thing twice more as fast as he could work the lever action. In the distance, the Apaches struggled to bring their ponies under control, with little positive results.

Upton hurried to his horses, untied their reins from the trees where they'd been hitched, mounted up, and rode away. He knew the Apaches had seen where he fired from and would be coming as fast as they could to catch him. That was the idea. By the time they got there and found his tracks, he would be a good distance away and covering up his trail. He was confident he could cover his tracks well enough to keep from being caught.

He planned to make a long circle and come back to the valley. Once there, he'd pick up Bishop's trail and follow it. The Apaches would be off looking for him, trying to catch him and make him pay for killing one of them.

26

Over the next two days, Bishop and Angelina stayed in the shallow cave. Bishop's wound was more painful than it was serious aside from the blood he lost. The bullet hit the outside of his left thigh and bored just under the skin for about six inches before exiting. Only a few inches more to the right and he would've been in serious trouble. Fortunately, he healed quickly. Good food, clean bandages, and the mountain air all contributed to his healing. Two days after being shot, he was able to put a little weight on the leg.

"I wish I knew for sure if it was Potts and Greer doin' the shootin' back there." This was a discussion they'd had several times over the two days.

"It just about had to be them," Angelina said again.

"You said there were two rifles firing, and they didn't belong to Apaches."

"That's right. The only other two people in the area that we know about are Potts and Greer. I didn't think Potts was mad enough at me to ambush me. Especially with Apaches around."

"Gold does strange things to people. Some of them seem to lose all ability to think straight when there's gold they think is theirs. They do whatever they have to in order to get it, no matter what happens to anybody else."

Bishop was silent for a few moments then, thinking about all that happened. "I know you're right, Angelina. Potts had to think that I knew where that canyon filled with gold was and that I wasn't goin' to share it with him. He said as much back there on the bench."

"We have something else that we have to face now, too. We are running out of food. When we had to run away from that ambush, one of the shots must have hit a rope holding one of the packs on the horse. We lost some food along the way here. We have enough for maybe two more meals."

Bishop took this in. It only took him a minute to know what he had to do. "Okay. I'll go huntin'. Those Apaches are prob'ly around on the other side of the mountain by now. They either lost interest in findin' us, or got busy doin' somethin' else. I'll find somethin' and make sure I can get it with one shot. That should be okay. I can cover my tracks well enough to keep any Apaches from follerin' me."

"John, is your leg healed enough to do that? You don't want to hurt it again by doing too much too soon."

"I don't have much choice. We've got to have food. Besides, I'll be on Streak most of the time. It'll be okay. I'm goin' to rest for a little bit, then I'll head out. Should be back by dark."

A FEW MILES AWAY, Cruz sat on his horse in the cover of a pile of boulders looking out across a small clearing at five Apaches riding single file through the trees on the other side of the clearing. He'd been avoiding the Indians for a day, trying to get away from them and around to the other side of the mountain where he knew Bishop and Angelina were.

The day after he found the shelter he'd been using, he heard the Apaches coming along the tiny trail that led right to him. How they found the trail, he didn't know, but they were close. He barely managed to get out of the shelter and down the side of the mountain before they came to the shelter. Even though they found where he had been, he was reasonably certain they couldn't follow where he went from there. There was no trail, and the ground under the pines was dark and covered in needles. If they had found him earlier in the day, they would have seen the indentations left by his horse going down the mountain.

For the last day, it was as if they were playing tag or something with each other. Every time Cruz thought he'd lost them, they showed up somewhere close. So he had to take off again. Gradually, they had worked their way around to the opposite side of the mountain from where he needed to be.

Now, as soon as they passed the clearing, Cruz pulled his horse back from the boulders and started off to the south. He hoped to put some distance between him and the Apaches this time. If he could do that, he could get around the mountain and find Bishop and Angelina and not bring the Apaches down on them.

His growling stomach reminded him he hadn't eaten in a day. Rummaging around in the bottom of his saddle bag, he did find one piece of jerky left. It was a big piece, so he decided to take one bite at a time as his meals until the jerky was gone.

Gnawing off one bite, he let it sit in his mouth until his saliva softened it. Then he chewed for a long time, getting as much pleasure as possible from the act of chewing. The jerky wouldn't satisfy him, but at least it would be something in his stomach. He would be sure to drink a lot of water at the next spring or stream he found.

. . .

AROUND ON THE other side of the mountain from Cruz, Upton pondered on what he'd found. Or, rather, on what he hadn't found.

After slipping past the Apaches following his shooting one of them, he'd made a long circle and come back to the mouth of the canyon. From there, he found where Bishop and the woman had been ambushed. Blood on the ground showed him one of them, probably Bishop, had been hit. He then followed their trail down the valley. At the end of the valley, he lost the trail completely.

I never thought Bishop would be good enough to cover up his trail to the point of me not being able to find it. Upton looked around the side of the mountain from where he sat in the cover of the trees at the mountain's base. *What would I do if I was in Bishop's shoes? I'm wounded and possibly bein' chased by Apaches.* He thought about that for a bit. *I'd want to find a place where I could stay hidden and treat my wound. I'd need a cave or something like that. Where would I find a cave? It would have to be somewhere around here on the side of that mountain. I've just got to take my time and look for a promisin' place.*

27

After resting for an hour, Bishop slowly got to his feet, tentatively putting weight on his injured leg. At first, he wasn't sure he could manage the burning pain or that the leg would hold up. But the longer he stayed up on it, the stronger it seemed to get.

Whether it gets stronger or not, he told himself, *I've got this to do. We've got have meat, so I've got to huntin'. Once I get up on Streak, it won't be as much of a problem, but gettin' up and down are goin' to hurt like somethin' awful.*

There had been a couple of times during the war that he'd had to make himself grit his teeth and do what needed to be done in spite of pain from wounds. He could do that again. He had to do it again. Angelina was good at a lot of things, but she wasn't a hunter. Besides that, he knew he could keep away from Apaches better than she could.

"Are you sure you will be all right?" Angelina's face showed her concern.

Bishop put his arms around her and pulled her close. With one finger he smoothed out the lines between her eyebrows and on her forehead. He pushed the ends of her lips upward to make a half-hearted smile instead of a frown.

"I'll be all right. The leg's stronger now that I'm up on it. You've done a great job takin' care of me. I don't even feel weak anymore." That last was a lie, but one with the intent of making her feel better. "You won't even have to help me climb up on Streak."

"I still wish you wouldn't go. Something, some animal will wander by here before long. Then you wouldn't have to ride out."

"I wouldn't be able to shoot a deer or whatever that wandered by here. The Apaches could hear the shot and know right where we are. This way, I can ride out a few miles, shoot somethin', and get back here before the Apaches can figger out where I shot from."

"Do you really think you can do that? What if you can't get back on Streak? What will you do?"

"I'll tie myself to the saddle and let him drag me back here." Bishop grinned. "Don't worry. I ain't goin' to let anything happen to keep me from gettin' here to you." He held her tightly for a moment. "This hasn't been much of a honeymoon for you, has it?"

"It's been the best honeymoon I ever had," she replied with a sly grin. "But only because I've been with you the whole time." She hugged him once more, then stepped back. "You better come back to me, or I will come looking for you."

"I'll be back before you know it."

Bishop climbed into the saddle from the right side again. He was thankful that Streak didn't put up a fuss when being mounted from a different side. Whether or not he could use his left leg to boost himself up and into the saddle was an unanswered question. Once he got settled in the saddle, he thought he could handle the pain from his leg wound. But after Streak took a few steps, Bishop began to wonder if this was such a good idea.

But he was careful not to let Angelina see how much riding hurt his leg. He was determined to find them something to eat and bring it back to her. In his mind, that was part of his job as a husband.

Bishop rode slowly away from their shelter, not just because riding was painful, but also to keep a sharp eye out for Apaches. They hadn't seen any in two days, so he thought they were probably not looking for them. Maybe something else had gotten their attention and had drawn them away. Or maybe they were just waiting somewhere, waiting and watching for someone to move so they could see them. In either case, he didn't want to run upon them by being careless.

He had to be a little particular about what he shot. Something as big as a bear or an elk would be too much for him to handle with the injured leg. So he kept his eye out for signs of deer or even wild pig. Either of those would supply them with a lot of meat and would be something he could manage

Bishop rode for an hour before really beginning to hunt. He didn't want to be too close to their shelter when he shot, but close enough to get back there pretty fast.

He spotted plenty of deer tracks as he rode. Some of them seemed fresh to him, but he couldn't really tell.

I wish Cruz was with me. He's a lot better tracker than me and could tell how fresh those tracks are. He might even be able to follow the freshest tracks and find the deer. But he's not here, so I have to do the best I can. Just hope it's good enough.

He found a spot on a little ledge where he could look out over some of the mountain. There, he watched and waited, hoping to see something moving. For an hour, he watched, but nothing moved that he could see. Finally, he gave up and rode back toward their shelter, dejected that he hadn't found anything.

Bishop rode slowly back toward their shelter, still hoping to run across something he could take back to Angelina. He hated to return as a failure in her eyes, even though he knew that was only his pride talking.

. . .

WHILE BISHOP HUNTED, Cruz was doing the same thing. He'd found enough materials to make a rudimentary bow and some arrows. Hopefully, what he'd made would give him at least one shot at a deer before breaking.

He'd been sitting at the base of a large white pine tree since just before dawn. His horse was tied fifty yards behind him in a stand of cedars. The gnawing feeling in his stomach reminded him he hadn't eaten since the day before when his jerky ran out.

I guess I should be searching for Bishop and Angelina, he told himself. *But if I don't get something to eat before long, I won't have the strength to look for very long.* A glance at the shadows of the pines around him told him he'd been sitting there for about two hours. *I'll give this hunt another hour, then decide what to do.*

During the time he'd been sitting against the tree, Cruz had seen squirrels jumping from tree to tree going after the pine nuts they could tease from the cones. Sometimes, the patter of falling bits of pinecones from the squirrels reminded him of rain. A couple of times he'd caught movements out of the corners of his eyes, but could never clearly see whatever made the movement.

At the end of the hour he gave himself, Cruz sighed quietly and started to push himself up from the ground when another glimpse of movement came to him. This time, the movement was right in front of him about thirty yards.

He sank back to the ground and waited.

A couple of minutes later, he made out the shape of a doe feeding along the ground. She was still twenty yards or so from him. He wanted her to come closer, within ten yards or even less. That was about the limit of what he thought the effectiveness of his bow would be. His intent was to make a clean kill. No need to cause an animal to suffer.

He sat there, not moving, but keeping his eye on the doe. He knew there was probably a buck somewhere nearby, too, and both of them would be watching closely for any danger.

The doe stepped daintily closer by a couple of yards. Then the buck materialized from the trees behind her.

Cruz knew he had to keep an eye on both of them and not move when they raised their heads from feeding. He wasn't sure what they were feeding on, but was glad they decided to come his way.

Minutes passed while the deer fed a little closer to him. Cruz slowly lifted his bow to the point where he could draw it back and let the arrow fly without too much movement.

Finally, the doe was less than ten yards away. She fed along, head down, still stepping closer.

But the buck was becoming wary. He sensed something wasn't right. He lifted his head and stared right at Cruz for a long minute. Cruz didn't even breathe.

As soon as the buck seemed satisfied and lowered his head again, Cruz drew back the bow and sighted as best he could at the doe now standing about fifteen feet from him.

When he let the arrow fly, he knew it went right where he wanted it to. It struck the doe just behind the foreleg. She jumped straight up into the air, hunching her back, then ran for a short distance when her feet hit the ground again. He found her not forty yards away.

After thanking her for giving her life as was the custom of his Indian ancestors, Cruz skinned her, cutting off the backstrap to cook right away. He built a small fire and hung the backstrap on a green stick over the fire. It cooked while he finished the skinning.

That backstrap may have been the best he'd ever tasted. Once it was gone, he licked the grease off his fingers and put out the fire.

Now, I've got to go find Bishop and Angelina. I don't know how much food they had with them, so this meat might be really welcome. All I've got to do is stay away from the Apaches.

AT THE TIME Cruz shot the deer, Daniel Upton rode slowly along the edge of the trees, stopping every once in a while to scan the walls of the mountain that bordered the valley where the ambush took place. He'd already seen and searched two places where he thought Bishop and the woman might have sought shelter.

I know they're somewhere close, he told himself. *I can feel it. They wouldn't have gone far after Bishop gettin' shot. They had to stop someplace and take care of his wound, even if it was a slight one. They'd need a place that was hard to see, but would give them a place to watch from. I've just got to keep lookin'.*

He rode on another hundred yards and pulled his horses to a stop in the shade. While he could see the sides of the mountain, it would be hard for someone to spot him as long as he stayed still. His clothes and the color of his horses blended in with the shadows and trunks of the pines around him.

Upton used his nose as much as his eyes when he searched. He reasoned that anyone who had a camp nearby would have made coffee sometime that day. They would likely have a fire to keep the chill off, too. Either of those smells would be one he'd recognize.

That's the way he finally pinned down the fact that he was right. The distinctive smell of wood smoke drifted past him as he sat in the shade of the pines. He noticed his horse also caught a whiff and turned its head to the right as if looking across the valley. Upton decided that was the direction he'd go.

IN THEIR SHELTER, Angelina placed another piece of wood on the fire and set the coffee pot close to heat up the water.

John will surely want some fresh coffee to fight the chill of being out hunting all day. Whether he kills anything or not, the coffee will be good. If he does kill something, the fire will be ready to cook it.

She had never been frightened of spending time alone. But she had never been alone in an area where Apaches roamed, either.

I know this shelter is in a good place. And John will be back before long. So why do I feel so shaky?

Angelina had the feeling that something was about to happen. What, she didn't know. Several times, she'd had the feeling so strongly that she went to the front of the shelter and gazed out through the screen of bushes in front of it that made it so hard for anyone to see. Every time she'd seen nothing. Heard nothing. Birds had been singing, the wind had rushed through the pines and set them to moaning, but all that was normal. There was nothing out of the ordinary.

But the feeling didn't go away.

She walked to the back of the shelter to check on her horse. When she turned around to go back to the fire, a man stood at the entrance to the shelter.

Angelina gasped loudly.

"Sorry to scare you, Woman," the man said. "But you sure were hard to find."

She felt in the pocket of her riding skirt for her pistol,

then remembered it was lying on her blankets close to the fire. Just to the left of where the man stood.

"Who are you? Why were you looking for me?" She managed to keep her voice level, in spite of shaking on the inside.

"Well, I wasn't lookin' for you specifically. My name's Upton, Daniel Upton. I'm lookin' for Bishop. He's got somethin' I want. Somethin' I need. Where is he?"

She thought for a moment about lying to the man, telling him something that he would probably see through immediately. But she couldn't even come up with something like that.

"He went hunting. We are running low on food."

"Uh-huh," the man grunted. He glanced around the shelter. "Not a bad place you found here." He spotted a used bandage she had tossed over against one wall. "I thought he got hit. How bad is he wounded? Must not be very bad, for him to be able to go huntin'."

"It is his leg. Not a bad wound."

While she talked, Upton was looking around. "I don't suppose Bishop left that diary with you, did he? That would sure save me some time and aggravation."

"No," Angelina said. "He keeps the diary with him. In his saddle bags."

"Too bad he didn't keep it in his saddle bags the whole time. I would've had it by now. Did you know I came into your camp late one night and searched his saddle bags?"

Upton had a proud tone to his question. "I could've had it then if he'd left it there." He glanced around again. "All right. Pack ever'thing up. We're goin' for a little ride. I want to surprise Bishop, but I want it to be on ground of my own choosin'."

28

Cruz made his way cautiously back around the mountain toward the canyon where the ambush happened. On his way he came across signs of Apaches. Unshod horse tracks mostly, but in one spot he found where some had spent the night. At least five sleeping spots were clear there. So he knew the Apaches were still close.

I think the best way for me to try to find Bishop and Angelina is to pick up their trail where they were ambushed. I should be able to follow them without too much trouble from there. Gettin' away from that rifle fire, they weren't too worried about hidin' their trail. Later on, they would be, but I should be able to foller 'em even then.

It took him most of the rest of the day to get back around to the mouth of the canyon. He easily found where the three of them rode out of the canyon and where he'd stopped to get the rock out of his horse's hoof. From there, he found the place where Bishop and Angelina were when the shot came.

He also found something else. Unshod horse tracks showed him the Apaches began tracking Bishop, too. Also, he found another set of shod horse tracks following them.

That puzzled him. Who was that other rider on the shod horse? Was it whoever shot at them? He didn't think so, because there were two shooters. He'd seen them briefly as they left their hiding places on the canyon wall. It was another person.

It had to be that Upton feller Bishop told me about. He's trailin' Bishop and the Apaches. I've got to be doubly watchful. There are two parties out there I don't want to run into.

A little way farther, he found the place where someone shot one of the Apaches. His body had been dragged off by the other Apaches at some time, but the sign on the ground was enough for Cruz. He saw where the Apaches turned and ran off toward the side of the mountain away from the trail.

Who shot the Apache? Whoever did it had done him a favor by taking out the Apaches. Now, he only had to be careful not to run into Upton.

. . .

WHILE CRUZ WAS on his way to the canyon to pick up his trail, Bishop rode back to their shelter. He could smell the wood smoke as he approached, and thought about the hot coffee that he hoped Angelina had ready for him. He was pleasantly surprised that his leg almost didn't hurt at all. Even with a lot of riding that day, it was more of an ache than serious pain.

As he approached the opening to their shelter something didn't feel right. He'd expected Angelina to have heard him coming and to have been standing at the opening watching for him.

But nobody was there.

A few yards from the opening, he stopped Streak and dismounted. But he forgot about his leg wound and dismounted from the left side, putting his weight on that leg.

The pain that shot white-hot through his leg and into his spine almost sent him to the ground. As it was, he had to grab hold of the saddle horn to keep from going down. Streak turned his head to look at him as if to say, 'What's wrong with you?'

"I'm okay," he said softly. "Just don't mind me holdin' on to you until this leg stops hurtin'."

If he'd been planning to sneak up to the entrance to the shelter quietly, that wasn't about to happen now. With all of the noise he made trying to get off Streak, anybody inside would know he was there. Would know and would be coming out to see what was going on.

But nobody came.

That worried Bishop a lot more than he was worried before. He pushed back from Streak's side and pulled his Remington from its holster.

Angelina should've come out.

He cocked the hammer on the Remington and eased forward toward the shelter. Listening, he heard nothing. Not the sound of a crackling fire, not the stomping or blowing of the horses. Nothing.

A quick peek around the corner of the entrance showed him no one there. He darted inside, pistol ready.

Nothing. Not even the horses. All of their gear was gone. The fire was only glowing red embers.

Angelina was gone.

Where could she be? Why would she have left the shelter?

The answer to that last question was: she wouldn't. Not voluntarily, anyway.

Bishop looked around at the dirt that made up the floor of the shelter. He saw her boot prints and those of someone else. Someone bigger judging from the size of the prints he left.

Cruz? No. Cruz wouldn't have taken her away from a safe shelter.

Potts and Greer? No again. Only one set of tracks

besides hers.

That left Upton! Upton had somehow found them and took Angelina knowing Bishop would follow them.

He hurried outside and saw a welter of tracks close to where he left Streak. Examining the tracks, he soon found where they led away from the shelter. No attempt had been made to cover up the trail, either. That settled it. Upton wanted him to follow them and try to get Angelina back.

He wanted the diary. That was the only reason he was there. The only reason to take her. And he wanted Bishop to find them somewhere Upton chose.

The only thing Bishop could do was follow the trail and hope his skill was good enough not to lose it if Upton decided to start trying to hide it. And that would be just like him. Hide the trail to frustrate Bishop, make him nervous, make him more likely to make a mistake.

I sure wish Cruz was here.

But his partner wasn't there, so Bishop had the job to do by himself. The thing that would probably save him was that Upton wanted him to follow them, so he made no effort to hide his trail. Holding onto that, Bishop climbed into the saddle again. This time he remembered to mount up from the right side.

The trail led out to the edge of the valley. Bishop almost missed where Upton turned away from the canyon where the ambush happened. He'd been thinking about Angelina and what he'd do to Upton if he hurt her in any way. He'd gone several yards into the open valley before realizing he no longer saw their tracks.

All right, Bishop, he scolded himself. *You've got to get your head in this. It won't do any good for you to think about anything other than follerin' this trail. There'll be time enough once you catch up to Upton to think about what you want to do to him.*

Reining Streak around, he rode back to the last place he saw the tracks. From there, he quickly found the trail again.

Upton seemed to have a destination in mind. From what Bishop could see, the man wasn't hesitating or pausing to look around. The tracks led in a sort of straight line to the end of the valley, then made another turn to head up the mountain.

Before long, Upton's trail led Bishop to another game trail that wound around the mountain. Like those kinds of game trails did, this one followed the easiest path around the mountain.

Bishop followed the trail, watching closely for any place where Upton might have turned off of it, for what seemed like an hour. Finally, he rode over a slight rise in the trail and stopped.

No more than a hundred yards ahead of him was the opening to another canyon. This one was smaller than the one where Hightower lived. And the tracks he was following led right toward the mouth of the canyon.

· · ·

BEHIND BISHOP, back in the valley, Cruz rode on following the tracks he knew were Bishop's and Angelina's, as well as those he thought belonged to Upton. He found where the tracks led into a grove of trees. Once there, he saw that Bishop and Angelina had stopped there, probably to bandage Bishop's wound.

From there, he followed the tracks back out to the valley. Then he stopped.

With Bishop hurt, they're goin' to want to find some place to hole up and let him heal. The best place would be a cave or somethin' like that where they would be hid, but could still see out. He studied the opposite wall of the valley, then turned his attention to the one beside him. *I need to keep my eyes open for that kind of place. And they're prob'ly not goin' to go much farther from here.*

Knowing that, Cruz started his horse walking forward. Scanning both sides of the valley, it didn't take him long to find what he thought he was looking for. Searching the ground carefully, he found where the edge of a horse's hoof had left an impression beside a rock. A short way farther, he noted a freshly broken limb on a cedar sapling.

Somebody's been here recently, and I'll bet it was Bishop and Angelina. Looks like that place up on the side of the mountain is where they've stopped.

When he got to the shelter, Cruz saw all the tracks that had been left by multiple horses. He also found Streak's tracks. For several minutes he studied them, slowly putting together most of the story. A short search inside the shelter told him Bishop and Angelina had been there and that somebody had taken one or both of them out of the shelter.

By the time he finished examining the tracks, Cruz was almost certain that Upton had taken Angelina from the shelter and that Bishop was following them. Climbing back into the saddle, he set off following the clear trail.

Out in the valley again, he found where Bishop had missed a turn and had to back-track to pick up the trail again. He grinned at the thought of how much he would kid his friend about that after this was over.

He set off again, easily following the clear trail left by Upton.

SEVERAL MILES AHEAD OF CRUZ, Bishop studied the mouth of the canyon in front of him. After a couple of minutes of seeing nothing moving, he touched his heels to Streak's side and rode on down to the canyon.

He got no more than a few yards into the canyon before it opened up and he stopped. Only about twenty feet in front of him stood Upton holding Angelina in front of him.

"I thought you could find us," Upton said. "I tried to leave a clear trail."

"The trail was clear enough. I'd really like for you to let Angelina go."

"I'm sure you would. And I'll gladly do that as soon as

you hand over that diary. I want to know where the canyon filled with gold is. I've been follerin' you all around long enough. I don't think you're goin' to find it."

Bishop slowly dismounted and took the diary out of his saddle bag. Leaving Streak ground-hitched, he stepped away from the mule.

"This diary isn't going to be much help to you, Upton. It doesn't give any directions. In fact, it doesn't even say there was any gold found."

Upton chuckled, a sound like glass being shaken in an iron tube. "Do you expect me to believe that? I know Thompkins was in on finding the gold. And I know Sharpe planned to find it and hide it from me. Sharpe lost the map I gave him, and I don't remember what the map showed. So I also know Thompkins wrote down where they found the gold and where they hid it. He had to so they could come back and get it later. So I want that diary." He pulled his pistol out and pointed it first at Bishop, then at Angelina's head. "If you want the woman to live, throw me that diary."

"You know if you shoot her, I'll kill you in the next second. Then no amount of gold will help you." Bishop shrugged. "But like I said, the diary doesn't tell about any gold. But if you want it, you can have it."

As he said this, Bishop threw the diary high and hard.

When Upton reached for the diary with his left hand, he let go of Angelina. Immediately, she fell to the ground and rolled over to the left.

Upton grabbed the diary from the air and brought it down to his chest. Grinning, he brought his eyes back to Bishop. Then he focused on Angelina and began lifting his pistol to take a shot at her.

"UPTON!" Bishop shouted. As he did, he pulled the Remington from its holster.

Upton turned to face Bishop, his pistol coming up. His face tightened into a grimace when Bishop's first bullet hit him just above his belt buckle. When the second bullet burned through his belly no more than two inches from the first, his face registered surprise, then shock as he fell back on his butt in the dirt. For a few seconds, he sat there gazing at the blood soaking his shirt and pants. Then he fell over onto his side.

Angelina jumped up and ran to Bishop, throwing her arms around him and holding on for all she was worth. Bishop hugged her as he watched Upton to make sure he was dead.

At a sound behind them, Bishop whirled and pushed Angelina behind him.

"I almost got here in time to help," Cruz said. "At least, it wasn't too late."

Bishop grinned at him. "It's good to see you anyway." Then he grew serious. "I think we'd better get on out of here. Those shots are goin' to attract every Apache for miles."

29

Bishop, Angelina, and Cruz found a dry gulley and rolled Upton's body into it. Then they pushed the sides in and found rocks to pile over the body to keep the coyotes away from it.

"There's not much else we can do for him," Bishop said. "I don't know anything about him. Not even where he came from."

"And I didn't find anything in his pockets or saddle bags that had any address on it," Cruz said. "There's no way to find out where to send any notice about him. I wonder why he wanted that gold so bad?"

"Don't know," Bishop said. "He told me once he had to take care of legal trouble. Maybe it had to do with that."

They stood and stared at the resting place of the mysterious man for a few minutes.

"He must've been a lonely man," Angelina said. "So this is about all he'd expect."

They caught up the horses and got on their way off the mountain. "Do you know where we are on the mountain?" Bishop asked Cruz.

"I have a pretty good idea," Cruz responded. "We should be on the north side. If we ride around to the south, we can cut across that big plain and head east to Magdalena."

"It'll be good to be away from here. I'm ready to get to someplace where we don't have to be constantly watching out for Apaches." Bishop turned and smiled at Angelina. "And someplace where you and me can set up our own little house."

They rode on for a half hour or so, following a trail that wound around the mountain. There weren't any fresh tracks on the trail, so they felt reasonably safe following it.

Riding over a rise in the trail they came upon a clearing. When the three of them rode into the clearing from the north, Potts and Greer rode out of the trees to the south. The two men had rifles in their hands pointed at Bishop and Cruz. They were grinning as they pulled their horses to a stop.

"Well, well," Potts said. "Looks like we won't have to go lookin' for you three after all. You done rode right up in our laps."

"No need to point those rifles at us, Potts," Bishop said.

"We're headed off this mountain and back to Albuquerque. We found where Thompkins is buried and didn't find any gold."

"Now that's where I've got to disagree with you, Bishop." Potts patted the bulging saddle bag tied on behind his saddle. "We found some gold. Enough for the two of us, anyway. I was always doubtful about a canyon full of gold, but we found a little vein back there on that bench. Cleaned it out and filled up our saddle bags."

"Okay, you got what you wanted, and we got what we wanted. We can all head off the mountain and on back to Albuquerque. We can go together or our separate ways."

Potts shook his head. "Nope. You see, that's another thing I've got to disagree with you about. When you found Ernest's body, you might've found somethin' else. Like maybe some pages he tore out of that diary?"

Bishop couldn't help but show the truth on his face. How did Potts know about the missing pages?

Reading Bishop's face brought a smile to Potts'. "Yeah, I saw that some pages had been torn out of that diary when I first got it. But I didn't know what happened to 'em. So Ernest had 'em, huh? Did he write anything on 'em?"

"Yeah," Bishop said. "He wrote that you shot him in the back and left him for dead. I would've expected that from you, now that I know you better."

The smile vanished from Potts' face. For a moment, Bishop thought the man was going to shoot him right then.

He even brought the rifle up to his shoulder. But Potts took a deep breath and relaxed, lowering the rifle again.

"I could shoot you right out of that saddle," he said to Bishop. "But that's not what I've got in store for you. I'm goin' to shoot you in both knees and leave you right here for the Apaches or the bears and wolves, whichever comes first. Then I'm goin' to take the woman. We'll kill her, too, after a while. You can think on that while you wait for the Apaches to find you." He half-turned to Greer. "Shoot that half-breed. We can't take a chance on him if we just break his legs."

"Be glad to," Greer said. He turned to Cruz. "I've been waitin' for a while to kill you."

He raised his rifle, sighted along the barrel, and then was blown out of the saddle.

The shot took all of them by surprise. It came from Bishop's right in the trees at the edge of the clearing.

Five Apaches seemed to materialize from the shadows under the trees. All of them had rifles trained on the four people left standing.

They rode up close to the whites, their black eyes steady on the four. The one who seemed to be the leader said something in his native language, but none of the others understood him.

He then said something to one of the other Apaches. That man rode up to Bishop and searched his saddle bags. Then he searched Angelina's and Cruz'. Finally, he opened

Potts' and found the gold. He turned to the leader and must've told him what he found.

The leader responded to the one who found the gold. That man then swung his rifle and knocked Potts to the ground.

Then the Apache leader turned to Bishop and spoke again.

"Do either of you understand what he's sayin'?" Bishop said without taking his eyes off the Apache.

"Not me," Cruz replied.

"Let me try Spanish," Angelina said. "Maybe he understands it."

She spoke to the Apache in Spanish. The man's face didn't change, but there seemed to be a sparkle or something in the depths of his black eyes. He immediately responded in the same language.

"What did he say?" Bishop asked.

"I told him we were not here after the yellow rock, but looking for one of the men who were here before," Angelina said. "He said none of those men found any gold, but this one did. He meant Potts."

The Apache started talking again. When he finished, Angelina responded to him. Then she translated.

"He asked what we were going to do now. I told him we wanted to leave this mountain and return to Albuquerque to tell Mrs. Thompkins what happened to her husband."

"Why ain't he sayin' anything now?" Cruz asked.

"I do not know," Angelina said.

Before she could say more, the Apache began speaking again. When he finished, he turned his horse away from them and led the rest of the Apaches to surround Potts.

"We should start riding," Angelina said. "He told me we can go because we do not have any of the yellow rock. They will keep Potts."

Riding away, the three of them didn't look back. They all knew what it meant that the Apaches were keeping Potts.

They were a mile away when they heard the first scream.

They didn't stop riding even when night covered the wide plain they crossed.

30

A week later Bishop and Angelina walked into the restaurant where Cruz was waiting. Sitting down with him, they ordered apple pie and coffee.

"How did it go with Mrs. Thompkins?" Cruz asked.

"She was sad that she is now a widow, but I think she expected it, too. There were some tears, but she's going to be all right. She said she has a better job now. She's takin' care of runnin' the hotel that her cousin bought while we were gone. She's goin' to be all right."

Cruz nodded. "That's good. What do we do now?"

"I don't know about you," Bishop said as he turned and faced Angelina. "But I'm goin' to take my wife back to Santa Fe and set up housekeepin' with her for a while."

Angelina smiled at him. That smile that always melted

his heart. "What if somebody else needs you to find somebody?"

"They'll have to wait a little while. I want to enjoy just bein' with you for some time."

THE END

Made in United States
Orlando, FL
01 October 2023

37489765R00114